CAPITAL
PUNISHMENT

When a respectable Washington
Senator became involved
with a shady, but well-stacked
widow, his daughter decided
to take a hand in the matter
. . . Mike Shayne's, that is.

It wasn't like Mike to kill
romance, but it seemed
that this one was doomed
from the start. And when
Cupid's arrows turned out
to be .38 slugs—the ever-
loving end got a little
too close for comfort.

THE VIOLENT WORLD OF MICHAEL SHAYNE

Brett Halliday

A DELL BOOK
An original mystery

Published by
DELL PUBLISHING CO., INC.
750 Third Avenue
New York, N.Y. 10017

First Dell Printing
—November 1965

Printed in U.S.A.

CHAPTER 1
11:30 A.M.

THE BIG FISH BROKE WATER LESS THAN TEN YARDS FROM THE boat. After battling Michael Shayne for half an hour, it had begun to weaken. Shaking its head in a vain attempt to dislodge the hook, it twisted in the air and went under. The redheaded private detective spun the reel, his shoulder muscles rippling under his T-shirt. Totally absorbed in what he was doing, forgetting the problems and frustrations of the past forty-eight hours, he worked the fish in close enough for Captain Prideaux to reach it with the gaff. Together they brought it on board.

"It's a big one, Mike," Prideaux said.

"Yeah," Shayne said happily, stretching.

"Bait up again. There are plenty of nice sailfish left out there. And why not use a barb this time?"

"One's enough, Jean. Let's go home."

He hung the rod carefully on its brackets, then picked up the cognac bottle and kicked a canvas chair around to face the rail. Maybe he could get some sleep on the way in.

At a sound behind him he turned, to find a blonde in a black sleeveless dress watching him from the cabin doorway.

"Congratulations on your fish, Mr. Shayne," she said.

Shayne swiveled around toward Captain Prideaux, who had suddenly become extremely busy disposing of the sailfish.

"What's going on here, Jean?"

The girl said quickly, "Don't blame Captain Prideaux. It's my fault."

Her heel caught as she stepped out on deck. Balancing herself, she took off her high-heeled shoes. She was good-looking in a chilly, self-possessed way, with well marked cheekbones and cool gray eyes. She was in her late twenties

5

or early thirties. The black dress, although simple enough, was far too elegant for a fishing boat. She brushed back her hair and laughed ruefully.

"I'm Trina Hitchcock. I have something to talk to you about, and Jean told me to wait till you'd caught a fish and put away a few slugs of cognac."

"That was good advice," the redhead snapped. "How much did you pay for it?"

Prideaux looked around angrily. "OK, so I was wrong! I disturbed the great man when he wanted to be alone. I apologize. Listen to her for a minute, will you?"

"No," Shayne said. "And the next time I charter your boat for a morning's fishing I'll look in the cabin to see who you're hiding. If there is a next time."

"I know this is terrible," the girl said. "I read about what happened yesterday, and you certainly deserve a day off. But I don't know what else to do!"

"I suppose you need a detective?" Shayne said.

"I certainly do! And if you'll just—"

"All right," Shayne interrupted. "If you saw the papers, you know I've been moving steadily for two days and two nights. That includes one eight-hour session, from midnight to eight A.M., with Petey Painter, Chief of Detectives on the Beach. He's never satisfied to be told anything once. He has to hear it a dozen times before he believes it, and after one of those nights the only way I can feel human again is to get out in the Stream, where there aren't any narcotics hustlers or stick-up men or Painters. Just fish. Now I'm going in and have a steak and a few drinks, and sleep approximately sixteen hours. I'll make a deal with you, Miss Hitchcock. Or is it Mrs.?"

"Miss. Or why not just Trina?"

"If you'll sit down and keep your problems entirely to yourself, I'll pour you a drink of good cognac and when we get in I'll give you the phone number of a reliable man who'll take care of you without charging you too much. If you still want to talk to me about it, call my secretary and make an appointment. I won't be in tomorrow, but I may be in the day after that."

"It can't wait that long, Mr. Shayne! And it has to be you."

"I'm sorry," the redhead said.

Prideaux returned to the wheel, and threw it over so hard that the girl took several quick steps and banged against the rail.

"Goddamn it, will you stop playing games?" Shayne yelled.

Prideaux came all the way about and headed back toward open ocean. He looked over his shoulder.

"And if you want me to turn around again you know what you'll have to do. You can probably take me, but if you're as tired as you say you are, you'll save yourself some trouble and listen to this girl. I've known her since she was a kid. Her daddy's the senator, Senator Hitchcock."

Shayne swore to himself savagely. "One of these days you're going to lose a customer, Jean, I mean it." He unfolded another canvas chair for the girl. "I'll listen, Miss Hitchcock, but that's all I'll do. And let's hope it isn't anything complicated."

She settled herself in the battered chair and called to Prideaux, "Thanks, Jean, that was noble. You can turn around now."

"Don't pay any attention if he growls at you," Prideaux said. "The whole thing's an act."

"Like hell it is," Shayne growled. "How's your father?"

"He's fine. Glowing, in fact, and that's the trouble. Mr. Shayne, I'm dying for a cigarette. I didn't want you to see smoke drifting out of the cabin."

Shayne shook out a cigarette for her and took one himself. He was trying to remember what he had read about her father recently. Emory Hitchcock, after several terms as a congressman, was now in his second term in the Senate. One of the least aggressive men in Washington, he rarely made the headlines. Shayne distrusted most politicians and kept as far away from them as he could, but he liked what he had seen of Hitchcock. The Senator had done him a favor once during an argument he was having with the FBI. Nobody wins arguments from that Bureau without important backing, and Shayne had needed help from Hitchcock to gain his point.

He snapped his lighter shut after lighting their cigarettes. "I said I'd give you a drink, but what are you going to drink it out of?"

"I can drink from the bottle. Really."

He looked at her skeptically and held it out. She hesitated, then put it to her mouth and took a long pull. She coughed most of it over the rail.

"Goodness, it burns! I admit it's the first time I ever tried that."

Shayne laughed. He drank from the bottle himself, corked it, and set it on the deck between the chairs.

She said, "I really hate to do this to you, Mr. Shayne. I know you'd like to throw me overboard and make me swim home, and that's what I deserve. Your secretary finally broke down and told me you were going fishing, and where I could intercept you. But she didn't hold out much hope that I could talk you into doing anything. She's nice, isn't she?"

"Damn nice," Shayne said.

"And after that I had quite an argument with Captain Prideaux before he'd let me aboard. Well—maybe all you can do is give me advice. God knows I can use it."

"Go ahead, Miss Hitchcock. If you see me falling asleep poke me."

She drew hungrily at her cigarette. "It's about my father, of course. A perfectly awful woman has her hooks in him. And when I say she's awful, I mean *awful*. He's nearly sixty. Fifty-eight, to be exact, and this can't be the first time in history someone his age has made a fool of himself over that obvious type of woman. If that was all there was to it, an older man in the clutches of a flamboyant younger woman, I don't say I'd *like* it, but I'd keep my mouth shut in the hopes that it would blow over. He's not just any fifty-eight-year-old widower, however. He's a United States Senator. What's happening is quite clear."

She colored slightly. Without looking at Shayne she said quietly, "They're trying to get a photograph of the two of them together in bed, so they can blackmail him with it."

8

"Who are they?" Shayne said.

"There's no mystery about that. The man who's behind it is named Sam Toby. I don't know how famous he is outside Washington, but he's famous enough there."

"Sam Toby?" Shayne scratched the reddish stubble on his chin. "Isn't he some kind of lobbyist?"

"On a high level. He's supposed to know where all the bodies in Washington are buried. He swung that big airplane contract last year—maybe you read about it."

"Sure," Shayne said. "That's what I was trying to think of. I remember there was a big stink at the time. I didn't bother with the details."

"It was actually quite simple. Six or seven companies were after the contract, but it boiled down to two. A billion dollars is going to be spent on that airplane, and even in Washington that's a lot of money. Sam Toby was pulling the strings for the underdog, and the underdog won. Daddy's subcommittee is trying to find out how he worked it."

"Tell me something about the woman."

"Her name's Margaret Smith. Naturally she calls herself Maggie. She's either a widow or divorced, there's no Mr. Smith that anybody knows about. She runs a little theatre, the kind that shows those strange offbeat plays about how hopeless life is. Well, you know what my father is like. Would you believe he could fall for a vulgar woman with a tumbled shock of artificial red hair, a bosom like the prow of the Queen Mary, a loud raucous laugh, powerful perfume, too much jewelry? And I'm only hitting a few of the high spots."

Anger had improved her somewhat frosty good looks, Shayne thought, but the most striking thing about this description was that it was the exact opposite of Trina Hitchcock herself. In spite of the stiff offshore breeze, her blonde hair stayed under control. Her voice was carefully modulated, with an accent that indicated an expensive New England education. There was a faint network of worry-lines around her eyes. Shayne doubted if she laughed much, and certainly she wouldn't ever be guilty of anything approaching a raucous laugh. He couldn't smell any perfume, she wore no jewelry except a single ring, and in addition to all this, she didn't have much of a bosom.

She seemed to guess what he was thinking. "I know I wouldn't feel so strongly if I wasn't his daughter. But the thought of *my father* having anything to do with that coarse woman makes me squirm. The first minute I set eyes on her I said to myself, 'So she thinks she's going to be the second Mrs. Emory Hitchcock, does she? Well, maybe. But if it happens, and I don't think it will, she'll know she's been in a fight.' And at the same time, you see, I felt a bit sheepish, because after all it's my father's own business whom he marries. *My* feelings don't count. Now that I know what they're up to I've stopped having qualms. Toby wants to get a weapon to make my father call off these hearings."

"Can he do that?"

"The whole subcommittee would have to agree, but he's been chairman for years and they usually do what he thinks is best."

"What makes you so sure she's working for Toby?"

"I did some detective work, Mr. Shayne. The whole thing seemed phoney to me from the word go. Daddy hasn't *looked* at another woman since Mother died. Naturally he's asked out a lot. There's a man-shortage in Washington, and he's never been a recluse. Heavens, far from it. But he hasn't paid attention to anybody in a romantic way. I live in the same house—I know. Then all of a sudden this. As soon as I got over being revolted, it struck me that there might be more to Maggie Smith than met the eye, even though what met the eye wasn't at all subtle. They met at a dinner before some kind of money-raising affair for her so-called theatre. I made a point of asking the hostess, very casually, you understand, how she happened to invite my father, as I'm sure he'd never set foot in that theatre, if he knew it existed. It turned out that Sam Toby had helped her make up the guest list."

Shayne started to speak. She said quickly, "I know that's not much by itself, but wait. They put her next to him at dinner and he never had a chance. The poor darling hasn't had much experience with that type of woman. She sewed him up fast. They've been seeing each other four or five times a week, and it's common knowledge now that he will not accept a dinner invitation unless she's one of the guests. It's even been in the papers, in a guarded way. I don't know if they've been sleeping together. He's behaving like a sentimental teen-ager, and at his age I don't think the symptoms would be that severe unless there was more to it than holding hands."

She was looking straight ahead at the white-flecked water running beside the boat. "I think I need another drink of that brandy. This is very—distasteful. But I want to be sure you understand the situation."

Shayne handed her the uncorked bottle. She was more careful with this mouthful, and much of it stayed down.

"I'm beginning to understand it," he said. "I don't understand why you think you need me."

"I need you *desperately*." She put her hand on his arm. "I've done everything wrong. I admit I didn't give her any benefit of the doubt at first—I was purely and simply appalled, and I let my feelings show. I said a few things to Daddy I probably should have kept to myself. We're still on speaking terms, but barely, and not on that particular subject. He's got some crazy idea that I'm jealous, which is absurd. If he wants to marry again, there's no reason he shouldn't, so long as the relationship has some meaning and isn't purely physical and temporary. But when a well-known lobbyist and fixer, under investigation by a senatorial subcommittee, sets up a blackmail situation involving the subcommittee chairman—well, he didn't let me finish. He hit the ceiling. He said he wouldn't stand for any interference in his private affairs. Interference! After all those years in Washington, he's amazingly naive. He couldn't see anything suspicious about that dinner invitation. I'm stymied, just when I'm on the verge of getting some concrete evidence."

"Concrete evidence of what?"

"Of the Smith woman's connection with Toby. She's carried out similar assignments for him before, it seems. This comes from an investigator who used to work for Daddy's subcommittee, a not very pleasant character named Ronald

Bixler, and he's going to want money before he supplies any details. And then what? Daddy won't listen to one single word from me against that woman."

"Then you'd better handle it from the other end," Shayne said, thinking. "Show the woman your evidence and tell her to lay off your father unless she wants to get herself in some real trouble."

"I'd be terrified! And trust me to mess it up somehow. If Daddy ever found out—and she'd make sure he found out—he'd always hold it against me. Nobody likes to have it proved that they've been behaving like an idiotic child. If it could only be managed so he wouldn't know—but I couldn't do it, I'm too involved."

"There must be somebody in Washington who can handle it for you."

She shook her head quickly. "That's the point. There isn't anybody I could trust. This is loaded with political dynamite. I couldn't give any local person that kind of hold over Daddy. How could I be sure they wouldn't betray us to Toby? Half the private detectives in Washington have done work for him at one time or another. No, it has to be somebody from out of town. And there's another factor. If anything does go wrong and you have to talk to Daddy about it —it won't, but if it does—I know you can make him listen to reason. He has a high opinion of you."

"I doubt if he even remembers me."

"You're wrong! He knows about all your big cases. And there isn't time to get anybody else. It has to be done today."

Shayne gave a half-grin. "Miss Hitchcock, I admire your father and the fact is that I owe him a favor. But I'm going to cork off forty-five minutes from now and you couldn't wake me up with a brass band. If you can wait till tomorrow, maybe. Otherwise—"

"Mr. Shayne! I know this is unfair, but it's so important. You can sleep on the plane. There's a two o'clock jet, and I think we can make it. I can phone Bixler from here and have him meet you at the airport. That conversation shouldn't take more than ten minutes. Then Maggie Smith, maybe half an hour. After that you can go to a hotel and sleep as long as you like. I'll pay you a thousand dollars."

"Not that I'm going to do it," Shayne said, "but what makes it so urgent?"

"Because tonight is when it's going to happen! Sam Toby has been subpoenaed to appear at the hearing tomorrow, so doesn't it stand to reason that tonight's their deadline? Daddy has a date with her, needless to say. He's picking her up at the theatre and taking her to supper at a fancy restaurant outside of Pine Grove. I heard him make the reservations. And that happens to be not just a restaurant but a motel." She hammered her knee with her fist, and there were tears in her eyes. "You know how these things are worked. Do I have to draw you a diagram?"

The redhead sighed and checked the level of cognac in the bottle. No, she didn't have to draw him a diagram. He had done very little anti-blackmail work in recent years, but this kind of operation was fairly standard. Toby would spend some money at the motel. When Hitchcock asked for a room, there would only be one vacancy, and the infrared camera would already be in place over the bed.

"OK," Shayne said heavily. "I hope it turns out to be as simple as it sounds, but we probably can't count on it. Forget about the fee. I was out of the country last election and I didn't have a chance to vote for your father. This'll make up for it."

"If you knew how much I've been counting on you! God, if you'd said no I don't know what I would have done."

"Now what's the guy's name again who has the information?"

"Bixler, Ronald T. Bixler. He works for the Civil Service Commission now. About how much to pay him. He must know how important this is. Do you think ten thousand would be too much?"

"Much too much. You have to be careful with these people, or they get inflated ideas. He'll want it in cash."

"I expected that. I have ten thousand dollars in a dispatch case at the Washington airport."

He looked at her sharply and she said in a quiet voice, "I knew I'd persuade you, Mr. Shayne. You see, I had to."

Shayne looked at his watch. "We're cutting it close. If that two o'clock flight is crowded I don't think we'll be back in time to get space."

"Oh, that's taken care of. Your secretary's making the reservations, and she'll be at the airport with your overnight bag and a clean shirt. She knew you'd say yes."

Shayne drank from the bottle and said dryly, "I appreciate being allowed to make up my own mind."

CHAPTER 2
2:00 P.M.

THEY BOARDED THE PLANE WITH TEN MINUTES TO SPARE, too late to find seats together. That was all right with Shayne. He knew Trina Hitchcock had told him all she intended to at the moment, and he hoped it would prove to be enough. He fell asleep wondering about the ten thousand dollars. Where had it come from?

A stewardess shook him awake, to tell him to fasten his seat belt. He stretched all over, putting a strain on the narrow seat, which had been built for a much smaller man.

Trina smiled from across the aisle. "I've never seen anybody sleep quite that hard."

"It didn't go on long enough," Shayne said.

He put a cigarette in his mouth, lighting it in the mobile lounge as soon as it had fastened itself to the great plane. The plane emptied and the lounge moved across the asphalt to the arrival building.

Trina, beside him, said in a low voice, "Now we have to start being careful. In many ways Washington is the smallest town in the world. Probably it wouldn't matter if anybody saw us together, but let's not chance it. The money's in a locker, and I'll give you the key. Use as much as you need, but of course I hope you'll have some left over. And I've been thinking: maybe you ought to offer some of it to Mrs. Smith, to make absolutely sure? What do you think?"

"I'm still half-asleep," Shayne said. "Let's see how it goes."

"I know you'll be playing it by ear, pretty much. I just thought I'd mention it. The first thing is Bixler. I don't see why he couldn't meet you some simple place, like here or your hotel room, but if he wants to be melodramatic we'll have to do it his way. He sounded terribly impressed on the phone when I told him he was going to be meeting Michael Shayne."

"Fine," Shayne commented. "Maybe he'll cut his price."

"Oh, I doubt that. You'll call me? I'll be home all evening."

Shayne nodded.

"Then good luck, Mr. Shayne." She put out her hand, looking at him directly, and let something personal come into her eyes for the first time. The worry-lines had deepened, but what she seemed to be worrying about now was whether he liked her. The tip of her tongue appeared briefly between her lips. All she said was, "I can't tell you how grateful I am."

Swallowing a yawn, Shayne watched her click off through the crowd. She looked more at home in this setting than she had on the deck of Captain Prideaux's charter boat. He checked the number of the key she had pressed into his hand, found the locker, and took out an almost-new dispatch case. Then he rented a new Ford and drove to the St. Albans, the airport hotel. After checking in he bought an afternoon paper and went up to his room to shower and shave. He was glad to see that Lucy Hamilton, his efficient secretary, had packed a fifth of cognac.

He poured himself a drink and counted the money. It came to ten thousand even, mostly in fifties and twenty-fives. He sorted out two thousand dollars, wrapped it neatly in newspaper, and snapped a rubber band around it. He put the rest back in the dispatch case. It was too large a sum to leave in his room, and he checked it downstairs before going out to pick up his Ford.

He wheeled in beside an empty taxi at the cabstand in front of the hotel. "I want you to show me the way to Rock Creek Cemetery," he told the driver. "Will two bucks cover it?"

"As far as that goes," the driver said. "You want to go in your own car? OK, it's your dough."

The driver took his money and drove off, with Shayne following closely. The other times he had been in Washington, his business had always kept him close to Capitol Hill.

He watched the street signs, but he didn't expect to be here long enough to learn his way around. He had to buy some information and deliver a message. That was all.

They were driving south on North Capitol Street when the driver in the taxi ahead blinked his directional signals. He pointed out the open window, turning all the way around to be sure Shayne understood, honked twice, and then pulled away. The redhead began looking for a place to park, and found one within a block. He locked up and walked back to the cemetery. He was a minute ahead of the time Trina Hitchcock had appointed with Bixler when she called him from the Miami airport.

Bixler's instructions, delivered in a muffled whisper, had been for Shayne to meet him in front of the famous Saint-Gaudens statue, "Grief." So that Shayne would recognize him, he had promised to carry a paperback copy of one of Michael Shayne's own adventures, put into novel form by Shayne's friend Brett Halliday.

The cemetery was a big one, crowded with memorial statues, fine trees and clumps of tourists, most of them busy taking pictures of gravestones. Shayne strolled toward the spot where the largest crowd had collected, and in a moment saw a great bronze figure of a seated woman, in a grove of evergreens. Bixler, on the fringes of the crowd, was nearly as conspicuous as the statue itself. Shayne could have identified him even without the paperback book, which he was holding awkwardly, so no one could miss seeing the front cover. He wore a three-button suit with all the buttons buttoned, dark glasses and a hard straw hat. He had a round face and a gray complexion, as though he spent his days indoors under fluorescent lights in air-conditioned buildings.

He saw Shayne at once. Shayne turned on his heel and walked away, letting Bixler overtake him.

"On the dot," Bixler said breathlessly. "I like punctuality. It's getting rarer and rarer. I was worrying about not recognizing you, but I knew who you were right away. You look exactly the way I expected."

"You can get rid of the book now," Shayne said.

"I'm certainly not throwing it away, if that's what you

mean." He stowed it in his hip pocket. "I'm not finished with it. I thought afterwards it was a mistake, a bit too much, because somebody might notice it and look at you and do a double take. I don't mind telling you I was flustered on the phone. This is a grand moment for me. I've always hoped our paths could cross someday."

"Where do you want to talk?" Shayne said. "I could use a drink."

"Oh we couldn't go to a bar," Bixler said. He had a slight lisp when he talked fast. "That's the wortht pothible place to transact confidential business. I could suggest sitting in my car, but I want to be fair—you couldn't be sure I hadn't bugged it, could you? And the same could be said for your car, looked at from my point of view."

Shayne's ragged red eyebrows came together impatiently.

"You don't know Washington," Bixler said. "Maybe you can get away with being slapdash in places like Miami, but this is the counterintelligence capital of the world. Maybe Miss Hitchcock didn't tell you how much money is involved. One billion dollars." The sum pleased him so much that he repeated it. "One—billion—dollarth."

"I hope your price is going to be lower than that."

"My word, yes! I'm not in that bracket, not by a long shot. I'm the low man on the totem pole, and to tell you the truth, that's how I like it. Nobody's been killed yet to my knowledge, but some violent people are mixed up in this and, with a billion dollars at stake, who knows what can happen? Let's just sit on one of these benches. You pick, and then you can be sure there's no recording device planted underneath it. OK?"

Shayne motioned to a backless stone bench. "Does everybody operate like this up here?"

Bixler looked around carefully before sitting down. "If they want to survive. I'm not afraid of being followed. I'm an old hand, and there isn't a tail in the business who can stick with me if I really want to lose him. The thing I worry about is coincidence. That's the trouble with going to a bar. *Anybody* can be in a bar. But nobody comes here but tourists."

18

"Maybe you'd better show me what you've got on Maggie Smith and then we can talk about how much it's going to cost."

"Show you!" Bixler exclaimed. "I have nothing to *show* you. I wouldn't think of making copies of confidential file material. This has to be entirely verbal. I thought I made that clear to Miss Hitchcock."

"Then let's hear it," Shayne said, trying to be patient. "But if you don't have any documentation it's going to affect the price."

"No, excuse me," Bixler said. A group of nuns approached, and he remained silent until they were out of earshot. "You have your methods, and I won't deny that they work, nine times out of ten. Even ninety-nine times out of a hundred. I wish I could be as free and easy as that, but I can't. I'm on a payroll. I have to charge you—" he glanced at Shayne quickly—"eight thousand for what I'm going to give you, so let me fill you in with a little background to justify the amount."

Shayne laughed easily. "Never mind."

"What do you mean, never mind?"

"We're in no hurry. I'm at the St. Albans. I might go as high as fifteen hundred, depending on how solid the stuff is, but that's where it stops. Call me if you change your mind."

"You're in no hurry!" Bixler said as Shayne stood up. "Mr. Shayne, I'm sorry to have to say that I don't think you understand this at all. Miss Hitchcock didn't fly to Florida and back because she's in no hurry. Why quibble?—it's not her money, they'll just charge it off to miscellaneous and collect from the government. Sit down. Please don't argue. Make it six thousand."

Shayne pulled at his earlobe, studying the anxious little man. "I don't like to buy a pig in a poke."

"I appreciate that. What I mean is, you're not just buying an episode out of a file. You're buying my know-how. Would you agree to that as a statement of principle?"

Shayne sat down. "Go ahead. I'm listening."

"Senator Hitchcock, Maggie Smith, Sam Toby. That's the sequence. I know the Senator well. I worked over two years for his subcommittee. He was a very good boss. As a matter of fact, I was running down a lead on Sam Toby a year ago when I got the Civil Service Commission offer, at a big jump in grade. That's not the coincidence it sounds, because we were always trying to prove something on that son of a bitch, excuse the expression. The man who puts Sam Toby out of circulation is going to be made. But it may not happen in my time. He's cagy. He's tough. He's slippery as an eel. Well, I always comb the society columns because you never know what you'll find. I read where Senator Hitchcock went to an opening at the National Theatre with somebody named Maggie Smith. A week later they were both on the guest list at so-and-so's dinner. I said to myself, 'Who is this woman? The name rings a bell.' "

"Miss Hitchcock says she used to work for Toby," Shayne said, trying to hurry him up.

"Maybe she said that," Bixler said. "I never did. I stick to facts and let other people draw the conclusions. I have a phenomenal memory for names. I fed Maggie Smith into the Bixler computer." He tapped his forehead, to show where the Bixler computer was located. "Nothing came out. I tried Margaret Smith. Yes! I looked it up and verified it. A Margaret Smith applied for a job with a theatrical company that was going overseas for the State Department, and we ran a routine check on her. We turned her down on grounds of moral turpitude, and Sam Toby's name was mentioned."

"In what connection?"

"This was eight years ago. One of his clients—call it Company X—needed a decision out of a certain administrative agency. The key man on the decision was Mr. Y, and Mr. Y's decision was no. Toby introduced Mr. Y to Maggie Smith. They went off on a joint vacation in the Caribbean. When they came back, Mr. Y canceled his no decision and made it yes. Those are the facts."

"Is this all on the record?"

"It's *in her file*. You can't expect documentation on a deal like that. Toby didn't get where he is by putting things in writing. The way we do—we get this kind of story on strict condition that the source isn't named. But the agent gives the source a believability rating. This one was excellent."

"I still don't know what I'm buying," Shayne said. "Eight years ago—it's pretty stale. Your anonymous source was obviously trying to damage the woman. The whole thing sounds very flimsy."

"How can you say it sounds flimsy?" Bixler exclaimed. "It wouldn't stand up in court, but that's not how it's going to be used. You'll notice she didn't get that State Department job, and they didn't have to give her a reason. They just said no. I'll tell you what you're buying, Mr. Shayne." He ticked off the points on his fingers. "The name of Sam Toby's client. The date. The real name of Mr. Y. The name of the cruise ship and the cabin numbers. I don't have to tell *you* what to do with that kind of information."

"I don't know my way around in this town," Shayne said mildly. "I'm open to suggestions."

Bixler said suddenly, "Would it be all right with you if I call you Mike?"

"Go ahead, if you feel like it."

"And it certainly would mean a lot to me if you could see your way clear to call me Ron. Well—if I can be of any assistance, I want you to know it would be an honor. It's true, I'm not exactly a novice."

He drew a deep breath. "What we want to do is to give this Maggie Smith a scare she won't forget in a hurry. Right? That Caribbean trip was so long ago she probably thinks it's forgotten. When you broach it to her she's going to be startled, to say the least. It goes without saying that she'll make herself scarce as far as Senator Hitchcock is concerned. If you tell her to get out of town for a while, she'll get out of town. That's one way to use the material. What I say is, go on the offensive with it. Tell her that unless she cooperates you'll call her to testify in open hearing and bring out the full facts about her old Sam Toby connection."

"Unless she cooperates in what way?"

"By testifying that Toby hired her to see what she could get on Senator Hitchcock. It wouldn't hurt her reputation too much. There are ways she could put it. After she'd gone out with him a few times, she realized she was doing the wrong thing, and now she wants to defect. This would be very damn good for National. You can see that. That's why I don't think I'm swindling anybody when I set the price at eight thousand."

"Don't forget I've only been here half an hour," Shayne said. "National who?"

"National Aviation!" Bixler said, surprised. "They're the unsuccessful bidders. I didn't know you hadn't been briefed. That's where the eight thousand I'm charging you is going to come from. And that's why—"

Shayne cut him short. "I haven't been hired by any aviation company. I've been hired by Trina Hitchcock to do one thing—break up a potential blackmail setup that's aimed at her father. As soon as I take care of that, I intend to get a good night's sleep and catch a plane back to Miami."

He took out the newspaper-wrapped parcel containing two thousand dollars and tossed it into Bixler's lap. "Forty fifty-dollar bills. Maybe you could get more from somebody else, but that's what I'm paying."

"Now, Mike—"

"If you don't want it, I'll see if I can handle it without any names. I think I have enough to keep Hitchcock out of bed with the woman for at least the next few days."

Bixler sighed. "I don't suppose I blame you. The smaller the payoff, the bigger your fee. But under protest, under protest, because it really is worth a hell of a lot more."

He put the package away. "The real name of Mr. Y—"

Shayne took out an envelope to write it down, but Bixler was so horrified that Shayne agreed to abide by local custom and commit the names and dates to memory.

"One word more, Mike," Bixler said, after testing Shayne to be sure he had everything, "I can see why you don't want to get mixed up in the contract investigation. I just want to say that I have it on good authority that a contingent of pretty rough boys from Texas are in town." He began ticking off points on his fingers again. "Manners Aerosystems, which won the contract, is a Texas company. If Toby put Maggie Smith on Hitchcock, and I think we can take that as proven, then Toby *and* Manners *and* these Texas gunmen, if that isn't too strong a word, aren't going to stand around with their hands in their pants pockets while you break it up. Do you follow me? That's why I personally have been watching my rear, and I advise you to do the same."

"Thanks," Shayne said.

"That's all right. If anything happened, I'd hate to think I hadn't warned you. I won't get up, and we'd better not shake hands. I certainly am glad I met you. I probably won't see you again this trip, but if you ever need anything done in Washington, I'm in the book."

With any luck, Shayne thought, that wouldn't ever be necessary. He nodded casually to the little man and walked away.

CHAPTER 3
5:45 P.M.

HE SPENT A HOT HALF-HOUR AND SEVERAL DOLLARS' WORTH
of dimes in a phone booth trying to track down Maggie
Smith. She could always be found at her theatre in the evening, he was told, but he wanted to be asleep by then. No
one knew her plans for dinner, but she had said she might
drop in at a cocktail party at the Swedish Embassy on
Sheridan Circle. Shayne rubbed his chin. Could he get into
an embassy cocktail party without an invitation? Probably,
and even if they didn't let him in, he could park nearby and
wait for Maggie Smith to emerge.

Enlisting another taxi driver, he found Sheridan Circle.
A fleet of parked limousines helped him identify the embassy. Two taxis were discharging passengers as Shayne arrived, after parking his Ford. After a moment's hesitation,
he walked up to one of the women, put out his hand and
said cordially, "Hello! Nice to see you again."

She gave him a brilliant smile. "How extremely nice to see
you."

Shayne went on, "I just got back this afternoon. Everything looks about the same."

"Oh, Washington never changes," she said. "It only gets
more so. You remember my husband?"

"Very well!" Shayne said heartily, and after another
handshake they all entered the embassy together.

Shayne's new friends gave their names to a servant in
livery in the entrance hall. Another servant checked them
off on a typed list. Shayne was clearly a member of the party.
The servant looked at him, but didn't ask for his credentials.

Inside, the noise level was already high. A waiter with a
large tray accosted Shayne and gave him a tiny glass of

colorless liquid, which proved to have the kick of the best moonshine whiskey, with a pleasanter aftertaste. He began looking around for a redheaded woman wearing too much jewelry and perfume, with the kind of coarse vitality that would attract a fifty-eight-year-old senator and horrify his daughter. He couldn't see anyone who even came close. There was a large buffet. Having eaten nothing all day but two hero sandwiches, Shayne loaded a plate, picked up another glass of the potent liquor and kept moving. Still he saw no one who would fit Trina Hitchcock's description of her rival.

Ten minutes later he arrived back at the buffet and refilled his plate.

"You must have a marvelous digestion," a woman beside him said approvingly.

"Only average," Shayne said, his mouth full. "Can I get you anything to eat?"

She was the handsomest woman he had seen so far, with dark hair and carefully made-up dark eyes. She was wearing a black cocktail dress with an extremely low neckline. A great deal of skin was showing, and it was very nice skin, Shayne thought, the color and consistency of thick cream. She was holding a highball.

"Can you get me anything to eat?" she repeated, shaking her glass. "There are too many calories in this. You *can't* be a Washingtonian. Nobody works up that kind of appetite in an office, and that's where all Washington males spend their time, without exception. I'm Adelle Redpath," she explained. "My husband's the Senator. I hate it when an attractive new man appears at a party and I don't know who he is. Now let me guess. You're not a politician, that's clear. You're not in the diplomatic service."

"Thank God," Shayne said. "I'm supposed to be meeting somebody, Mrs. Redpath, and if I can get through here—"

"You'll make yourself some enemies if you try," she said. "Face the fact, you're caught. I'm still guessing." She put one finger appraisingly to her lips. "If you were a mystery guest on a TV show, considering your height, those shoulders, those lean flanks, and let me see—the sun wrinkles at the corners of your eyes, I'd guess you're a private detective from Miami."

"This quiz is fixed."

"It is indeed. I was just talking to a congressman from your part of the world, Mr. Shayne. He told me your name and I've been stalking you ever since."

"Why?"

"This time you guess. No, that's not fair. From the way you're wolfing the smorgasbord, you probably haven't been in town long enough for a real meal. I don't want you to think I'm a mind reader, although as a matter of fact I've been complimented on my mind-reading ability, but you're looking for somebody named Maggie Smith, aren't you?"

Shayne had just taken a bite of an open sandwich, some kind of oily fish on a triangle of bread spread with pâté, and it stuck in his throat. He managed to get it down without choking.

Mrs. Redpath laughed. From a short distance, she probably looked lighthearted and carefree, but he was close enough to get other vibrations. The laughter was only on the surface.

"We're incurable gossips," she said. "When a widowed senator like Emory Hitchcock suddenly begins to be seen everywhere with a sexy widow, it excites comment. And naturally everybody's a bit tense about this lobbying investigation. Those things have been known to get out of hand. You're working for National Aviation, I suppose?"

"Mrs. Redpath, I don't know National Aviation from a hole in the ground," Shayne said truthfully. "I think there's an opening there. Excuse me."

"One more minute," she said softly. "I have a small interest in this. I introduced them."

Shayne turned. "Mrs. Smith and the Senator?"

"Yes. I asked him to a little dinner I was giving for Maggie's theatre, and that's where it seems to have started. Sam Toby's a friend of mine, a very old and dear friend, and he helped me make up the list. It was all very impromptu, not in the least sinister."

26

"I'm glad to hear it," Shayne said. "Can you talk a little louder? I'm only catching about two words out of three."

"This isn't the best possible place to talk. You may not realize how you stick out in this crowd. As it happens, my husband played a peripheral role in the award of this contract, a very minor and unspectacular role, and that's why I hope the hearings tomorrow won't degenerate into one of those name-calling brawls. Can you hear what I'm saying?"

"Barely."

She came closer, pressing her breast against his arm. "I can't expect you to take any advice from me. But what you'd better do, Mr. Shayne, is go back to Miami before the booby traps start exploding. Well, I know you probably won't. But I'd like to make you an offer. I've been finding my way through the Washington quicksands for too many years, and if you run into anything you don't understand, phone me. I won't promise I can give you the answer, but I might be able to send you to someone who can."

"That's generous, Mrs. Redpath."

She gave him a swift upward look. "It's not generous, and that's your first lesson. If your interests coincide with mine and my husband's, I'll help you. Trina Hitchcock talked to me. I could see what she thought—that Sam Toby hopes to use Maggie to compromise her father in some way. I doubt it. Whatever Sam is, he can't be accused of being crude. But if it turns out that there's anything to it, anything at all, I'll be miffed. I don't like to be used. Keep that in mind and take advantage of it. Will you recognize Maggie when you see her?"

"I think so."

"She's here. I'll point her out to you." She put her hand familiarly on his shoulder and came up on her toes to look around. "Yes, over there."

"Where?"

"In the beige dress. See the tall man with white hair and the monocle, talking to the President's wife? Maggie's—no, she just went out. You may be able to catch her in the hall. Now, remember what I said. Phone me, it doesn't matter how late."

"All right, Mrs. Redpath, thanks."

She maneuvered to one side and let him pass. The jam had become much worse. Halfway to the door he collided with the woman he had met on the sidewalk when he arrived. She, too, had been drinking the Swedish national liquor, and she gave a squeal of pleasure, recognizing Shayne. Their friendship had ripened very fast, and she now seemed to look on him as one of her oldest friends. He persuaded her that he couldn't possibly take her to dinner, and continued to work his way to the door. But she had delayed him too long. By the time he reached the sidewalk Maggie Smith was gone.

CHAPTER 4
8:25 P.M.

SHAYNE STOPPED AT A BAR FOR A COGNAC TO KILL THE TASTE of the open sandwiches. While he was there he looked up the address of Maggie Smith's Little Club Theatre. It was on Macomber Court. He hired a taxi driver to point it out to him, parked his rented car, and then had a hard time finding it again. Macomber Court was a tiny cobblestoned street, so narrow that he nearly walked past the entrance. The houses on it were two windows wide and jammed tightly together. Probably the theatre had once been a stable.

The first act was underway. In the ticket booth, a bony girl with her hair in a ponytail brightened at the prospect of selling Shayne a ticket. He grinned at her and stooped so she could hear him through the round hole in the window.

"Where do I find Mrs. Smith?"

"I'm not sure that she's here tonight," the girl said vaguely. "What do you want to see her about?"

"A friend of mine told me to look her up when I came to Washington. What do I do, walk in?"

The girl slid off her stool. "No, wait here. If anybody wants a ticket, tell them I'll be back."

Instead of going into the theatre, she went along the alley and around the building. Shayne looked at the posters while he was waiting. A local dramatic critic had called the play "a searing statement about our precarious human condition."

The box office girl came back. "Mrs. Smith was in earlier, but she's left for the night. Would you like to leave your name and phone number?"

"I don't want to chase her around town," Shayne said. "Could you get a message to her? This friend of mine met her on a Caribbean cruise. I'll write it all down."

Using the back of an envelope, he wrote the real name of the man the little Civil Service investigator, Ronald Bixler, had called Mr. Y, and added the name of the ship and the stateroom number.

"I'll see," the girl said uncertainly.

She went back around the building. Shayne had cut the fuse very short. Before the count reached ten the girl was back, bringing Maggie Smith with her. An unlighted cigarette in his mouth, the redhead watched them approach. Trina Hitchcock, thinking of Maggie in terms of a potential stepmother, had exaggerated some things and omitted others. Maggie Smith's hair was a dark burnished red. She wore it long, combed back from her forehead. A pair of horn-rimmed glasses had been pushed up out of the way. She was in her late thirties, Shayne judged, with a pleasant face and a humorous mouth. He had only an instant to appraise her, but that was time enough to realize what it was that had so frightened Trina. Physically Maggie Smith was one of the most exciting women he had ever seen. Her arms and shoulders were bare. It was true that she carried a great deal of jewelry—necklace, rings, bracelet, earrings—but what had seemed overdone to Trina seemed fine to Shayne. She wore a full-skirted dinner dress.

She looked at him curiously. "What you sounded like," she said in a throaty voice that went with everything else, "was a process server. I have a vast number of creditors, and some of them have begun sending me registered letters, I'm sorry to say. Thank you, Agnes," she said to the girl. "Better get back to the window. There might still be a few latecomers."

"I hope so, Mrs. Smith."

Maggie Smith lowered her glasses to read the address on the front of Shayne's envelope. "Michael Shayne, Miami, Florida."

"Are you busy?" Shayne said. "Can the theatre get along without you for half an hour?"

"I'm not exactly busy, but I'm working in a new actress in the lead, and I have to stay within shouting distance. I think I can squeeze you in backstage."

30

As they started around the building, Shayne remarked, "How's business, not so hot?"

"Business is lousy. We got rave reviews and the few people who've seen the play are crazy about it. I hope we can keep it open so it can find its audience." She glanced at him. "I really doubt if you'd like it."

"Thanks," Shayne said with a grin.

Her arm grazed his as they turned the corner, and he grounded some of the electricity she was carrying around. He didn't like what he had heard about her, and for her part, she must have known that he was bringing bad news. Nevertheless, the flow of current continued. It was something she obviously couldn't help, and she might not even know it was happening. It was simple, uncomplicated sensuality, and Shayne told himself that he had better drop his bomb fast and get the hell back to Miami.

They went up two steps and through a fire door that had been propped open. A thin actress with green eyelids, puffing almost desperately on a cigarette, flattened herself against the wall to let them pass.

"Where did you find *him*, Maggie?" she said.

"Never you mind. You concentrate on your lines. Don't hurry them tonight. Those pauses are vital."

She took Shayne into a small office, which had barely room enough in it for a littered desk and two chairs. The walls were covered with theatrical posters and autographed photographs. None of the faces in the photographs was familiar to Shayne. If they were famous, it was in a world he knew nothing about.

She closed the door carefully. "The good thing about this building is that it's solid. I can yell at you in here and nobody'll hear me."

Shayne cleared a corner of the desk and planted his hip on it. "Yelling won't help, Mrs. Smith." He took his unlighted cigarette out of his mouth. "I don't suppose smoking's allowed."

"Go ahead. It's against fire regulations, but maybe the best thing I can do for this theatre is burn it down."

His lighter flared. She picked a cigarette out of a pack by the phone, and let him light it for her.

She sat down behind the desk, first moving a small pile of bound typescripts. "If this is blackmail, I don't see how I can make it worth your while. I'm not just broke. I owe money all over town. Or isn't it money you want?"

"I want some cooperation, Mrs. Smith." He took the envelope from her and tore it into quarters, then dropped them in a heavy glass ashtray and set them on fire. "Is the name of the boat and the name of the guy enough, or do you want the rest of it?"

"I think I'd better hear a little more," she said evenly. "Because there's always a chance you're bluffing isn't there?"

"The man who arranged it was a fixer named Sam Toby. A corporation he was working for wanted a favorable ruling from the Wage-Hour Division in the Labor Department. The cruise lasted nine days. After you got back—"

"That's enough," she said. "I won't ask you where you got this because I know you wouldn't tell me. I just hope it's not in the public domain." She closed her eyes and pinched the bridge of her nose hard between her thumb and forefinger. "What do you want from me?"

"I want you to stop seeing Senator Hitchcock."

Her eyes opened. "So Trina sent you. I don't like to think unpleasant thoughts about anybody, but Trina Hitchcock is one person I think civilization could easily do without. I wouldn't have said she was your type, either."

"Few of my clients are," Shayne said. "I don't let it bother me."

"Are you a lawyer?"

"No, a private detective. She thought it would be better to have it handled by somebody from out of town."

Maggie hit the desk a hard blow with her knuckles. "I didn't think she'd go this far! I knew she didn't approve, she hasn't made any secret of that, but my God! Usually it's the *parent* who's possessive! Do you know how Emory has been spending his evenings the last few years? Bookbinding. That's a restful hobby, and he actually does very good work. But it's not too stimulating."

"I'm sure you're an improvement over bookbinding, Mrs. Smith."

"I want to tell you something. I don't know what's wrong with Trina, but sometimes I think it's fairly major. Her father is serious about being a senator. He works hard, and he's good at it. I don't agree with all his ideas, but they're his own and nobody else's. He's never made five cents over his government salary. He doesn't give a damn about popularity inside the Club."

"That's why I think he deserves a break."

"You *can't* think that. So long as he lets his daughter decide whom he can see and whom he can't, he's in danger of drying up, of turning into a self-indulgent, crotchety old man. I don't like to pat myself on the back, but he's changed in the last few weeks. He's started enjoying himself for the first time in years."

"You still don't get the idea," Shayne said wearily. "I wasn't hired to argue with you. We want this broken off, and it has to happen right away."

After a moment's silence, breathing out a mouthful of smoke, she said, "Tell Trina I said to go to hell."

"OK," Shayne said. "Any other message?"

"Mr. Shayne, look! He's beginning to break out of his cocoon. That sounds corny, but it happens to be true. How do you think he'll feel, or doesn't that matter?"

"Don't leave it up to Trina to tell him. Break off with him yourself and he won't have to know about those nine days in the Caribbean."

"Oh, it must be wonderful to be so sure you're right! Well, I'm going to fight you. This happened eight years ago, when I was a different person, and I think Emory will be able to understand that. I have a chance."

"Maybe, if it was between you and Hitchcock. But I'm in on it, and I'm here to make sure you lose. Unless you back out, and I mean as of now, I'll draw up a memo giving the full facts of that Caribbean cruise, and run it through the copier. I'll get Miss Hitchcock to tell me where to send the copies. Does your theatre have a board of trustees? That would be the logical place to start. And she'll have other ideas."

She stared at him. "It's too bad you didn't grow up in Germany. You could have had a wonderful career under Hitler."

"Never mind the remarks. First you say yes, and then we'll figure out how to make it stick. I think you'd better leave town for a while."

"You filthy bastard." She drew a deep shuddering breath. "You're right—I don't want that story circulated among my trustees. Oddly enough, I think I could explain it to Emory. He's a human being."

"I know it's been beautiful," Shayne said sarcastically. "And now it's over."

Her voice trembled. "I made a bad mistake once, and I've always had a sneaking suspicion I'd have to pay for it someday. Exactly what do you suggest I do?"

"Call him up and cancel your date for tonight. Say you have a headache."

"That's no lie." She lifted the phone slowly, as though it was heavier than she expected, and started to dial. Then she slammed it back and stood up. "No! First I think I deserve the privilege of telling you what I think about people like you. You're one of the main things that's wrong with this world, Mr. Shayne. Probably my friendship with Emory wouldn't have amounted to much. There were too many arguments against it. He doesn't care about the theatre and I don't give a damn about politics. But it was nice! After an evening together life seemed to be fairly manageable for a change. Do you think that *anybody*—anybody on God's earth, including detectives—has a right to any privacy?"

She was beginning to get through to him. "You've made your point," he said. "Now get on the phone. This isn't just anybody. It's a United States senator. Make the goddamn phone call and then you can yell all you like, if it makes you feel any better."

She said coldly, "What does the United States Senate have to do with the fact that a dried-up stick like Trina Hitchcock doesn't consider me a suitable playmate for her father?"

34

"Do you think I give a damn how many women he sleeps with if he isn't hurting anybody? But Sam Toby didn't dump you in his lap as a public service. Everybody keeps telling me there's a billion dollars involved here, and then they go on to say that a billion dollars is a lot of money. Just don't act too hurt. Make the phone call and get it over with."

She picked up the phone again and tried to club him with it. He caught her hand. She was breathing hard. As her breasts rose they almost touched him.

"Is that what Trina told you? That it's the same as eight years ago? I'm doing something for Sam Toby?"

"Come on," Shayne said roughly, "what difference does it make?"

"It might make a lot of difference. I want to know what kind of story she sold you."

"Will you get it through your head that we aren't just guessing? We know that Toby set up the first meeting with Hitchcock. That's definite, and it goes on from there."

"It isn't all that hard to meet people in Washington. We met at a dinner party. I don't think Sam was even there."

"But he arranged for Hitchcock to be there, and to be seated next to you. This comes from Mrs. Redpath. Why would she lie about it? The only thing we don't know is how much you're being paid."

Her face darkened. "I see."

"If he had to pay you anything. With this other thing to hold over you, he might be able to get you for nothing."

"Just so I'll know where I stand, what do you think I've been hired to do?"

"To frame the guy, for God's sake! You'd have a few drinks with supper. Then a few more. Then you'd make the famous remark about how it's been such a wonderful evening you don't feel like saying goodnight. Then one of you —Hitchcock himself, if the drinks and all those dreamy looks have taken hold—would bring up the subject of a motel."

"That's enough!" she said.

"And then tomorrow morning Toby would turn up in his office with the photographs, and naturally nothing would happen to him at the hearings. The thing that makes it perfect is that you don't look the type. But I have an idea you'd take a good picture."

"What type do I look, Mr. Shayne?"

She slid open the top drawer of the desk, felt in it as though looking for a pencil, and brought out a little automatic. It was a .25, a lady's weapon, but in Maggie Smith's hand it looked efficient and deadly. Her lips had tightened, and Shayne knew she was perfectly capable of pulling the trigger.

She held her right wrist with her left hand to keep the muzzle from wavering. "Don't move until I tell you to. We've had a rash of holdups around here, and my friends made me buy a gun. Now I have to think for a minute."

"You won't shoot me," Shayne said.

"Not even with a billion dollars at stake?"

"You're being dumb, Mrs. Smith. I know Toby won't like to be told that his plan has flopped. But he'll know you tried. If that gun goes off, you'll be in a real jam. Too many people know I'm here."

Her green eyes had filmed over. "If I shoot you, I'll think of something. I'm quite ingenious. But I'd try to shoot you in the shoulder, where I understand it hurts. I'd prefer to knock you unconscious. I have to talk to Emory before you do. Now I want you to keep those big hands away from your body and turn around slowly. You're a sizable target, Mr. Shayne."

Shayne eased carefully off the desk. "I'd like to tell you why I think this stinks before you slug me. Any kind of blackmail is bad, but this kind is really lousy."

She motioned impatiently.

"Sex is a fine institution," Shayne said, beginning to turn. "I hate like hell to see it being used this way. What did Hitchcock do to deserve it? He's just trying to do his job. I can tell from looking at you that you wouldn't be mixed up in this unless somebody was squeezing you. You don't need money that much. I've just had an idea. Tell Hitchcock the whole thing, and let's put Sam Toby in the can where he belongs. Then you can stop worrying about that old mistake in the Caribbean."

"Will you shut up?"

She shifted the gun to her left hand and picked up the heavy ash tray. Her tears had finally formed and spilled over. Shayne lunged backward, clamping the little gun between his hip and his elbow. She tried to wrench it free, and he stepped up the pressure. She brought the ashtray down hard on the back of his neck, a bad place to be hit. He twisted away, getting her wrist in one hand and shaking it with a wringing motion. The automatic went spinning across the room and broke the glass protecting one of the autographed pictures.

She brought the ashtray around again in a jangle of bracelets. She would have broken his jaw if she had connected. He released her abruptly. She hit the corner of the desk and the ashtray crashed to the floor. She came back at him, trying to rake his face with her fingernails.

"Oh, you bastard," she sobbed.

One of her fingernails grazed his cheek. He forced her arms against her sides. The perfume she wore was strong and disturbing. She tried to bring her knee up between them and he tightened his hold, bringing her in against him.

He held her tightly until she began to subside. He was getting her full charge. There were no two ways about it; this was a hell of a lot of woman. Suddenly her defiance left her. She rested her forehead against his shoulder. Shayne's tight punishing grip had become an embrace.

"Please, Mike," she said. "You're hurting me."

She heard the click of the latch before he did, and sprang back.

"Maggie?" a man's voice said. "Are you busy?"

IT WAS HITCHCOCK.

He was shorter than he looked in photographs. He was able to look dignified at times, but his face was constantly relaxing into a more natural expression. Shayne recalled that he was constantly running his fingers through his shock of iron-gray hair. He was famous for the sloppiness of his dress. His suits were rarely pressed, and they were usually sprinkled with ashes from the long cigar that was almost always in his mouth.

Tonight, calling on a lady, he was wearing a new gray suit. His shoes were shined, the knot of his necktie was in place, and his hair was brushed. He had a bouquet of roses.

"Maggie, I know I'm early, but I thought you'd be willing to skip Act Three for once. I'll wait outside."

"No, don't do that," Maggie said, touching her hair. "Senator Hitchcock, this is Mr. —" she hesitated "— Wayne."

Shayne's foot touched the little .25. He stepped aside, as though to give Hitchcock room, and kicked the gun under the desk. He was thinking quickly. They had met only once. The light was dim, and there was a chance that Hitchcock might not recognize him. He wasn't sure if his face was bleeding and he was careful not to touch it to find out. Maggie had more color than usual, and she was breathing too rapidly. More than that, the atmosphere in the room was still electric with emotion. Hitchcock must be aware that something had been going on.

"How do you do," Hitchcock said without looking at Shayne. He made a clumsy motion with the flowers. "Shall I leave these here or—"

"Emory, they're lovely," Maggie said automatically, taking them. "I tried to call you. I'm terribly, terribly sorry, but I'll have to take a rain check on tonight. I have a ghastly headache. The worst."

"My dear, I'm sorry," Hitchcock said, concerned. He sent a sharp glance at Shayne, looking for some connection between this tall, rugged stranger and Maggie's headache. "It's Mike Shayne!" he exclaimed. "I thought you said Wayne."

"Glad to see you, Senator," Shayne said gruffly.

Hitchcock put out his hand. He looked pleased for only a moment. His foot crunched on broken glass and his eyes narrowed. He looked at Maggie, then at the broken picture on the wall.

"What brings you to Washington, Mike?"

"It's a long story," Shayne said, improvising. "I've been trying to pick up some leads on one of our local hoods who's on the run. I was told that one of the actresses here used to shack up with him, but it turns out to be somebody else with the same last name."

This was the best he could do on a moment's notice, and he knew it didn't sound convincing. Hitchcock seemed to accept it. He nodded and turned back to Maggie.

"Maggie, dear, reconsider. It's tension that gives you those headaches, and right here in this building is where the tension starts. Come on, hop in the car. We'll put down the windows and let the wind blow it away. I thought we could go out to that place we liked in Pine Grove. Champagne's better than aspirin, and champagne and aspirin in combination are irresistible. If you don't feel like conversation, I'll keep quiet and just look at you."

"You make it sound wonderful, Emory." She closed her eyes again and pinched the bridge of her nose. "But I can't tonight. I'm going home and collapse."

"I confess I'm disappointed," Hitchcock said. "For selfish reasons. I won't be home a minute before the phone will start ringing—somebody from *The New York Times* wanting to know about the hearings tomorrow. The subject of Sam Toby is beginning to bore me stiff. Mike!" he said suddenly. "What are doing right now? Come home with me and I'll give you a drink."

"I'd like to, Senator, but I've got to hit a couple more places before I call it a night."

"One drink. I have some good cognac. I'd like to hear more about this hoodlum you're chasing."

"All right, sir. Five minutes, and then I'll have to duck out."

"Don't call me sir. I get enough of that on the Hill. Maggie, tomorrow night maybe I can talk you into skipping all three acts. They know their lines by now—let them stew in their own juice. Sleep well, dear."

He took her by the shoulders and kissed her forehead lightly. Her eyes caught Shayne's and skidded away.

"Emory," she said with difficulty, "there's a chance I may have to go to New York tomorrow morning. I'll phone you. Good luck with the hearings."

"No problem there," he said. "Sam Toby will prove to be a little too fast on his feet as usual and we won't lay a glove on him. What people don't realize is that just because everybody *knows* there's something fishy about that contract does not necessarily mean we can prove it. I've adjusted to that, finally, and it doesn't surprise me. It still seems to surprise *The New York Times*. Coming, Mike?"

Shayne followed. The Senator was out in the poorly lit corridor when Maggie whispered, "Mike."

Shayne stopped. She drove her knuckles viciously into his kidneys from behind. He drew in his breath sharply, and tried to smile as Hitchcock looked around.

"I hope your box office picks up," Shayne told her. "Sorry I bothered you for nothing."

"Are you?" she said.

Hitchcock had parked his black Lincoln in a no-parking space near the entrance to the alley. Shayne opened the door for him.

"I rented a car. It's around here somewhere, and I might be able to find it. I'll follow you."

Hitchcock reached into the back seat for the phone. "How much truth was there in that rigamarole you gave me about chasing somebody, Mike?"

Shayne tried a grin. "Not much, and I didn't think you

swallowed it. But I thought I was going to have a couple of minutes to myself to think up something better."

Hitchcock worked the dial in the base of the handset. He put the phone to his ear and waited.

"Trina?" he snapped. "Don't go out, please. I've changed my plans. I'll be home in a minute, and I'd like to talk to you."

He put the phone back without saying goodbye, and said to Shayne, "For the first minute and a half I thought I'd walked in on a clinch. It wasn't pleasant. Maggie is a very desirable woman, and I'm painfully aware of the difference in our ages. But that was anger I saw in her face, wasn't it? She'd just thrown an ashtray at you? I've been in this rough-and-tumble business long enough to learn how to look after myself. I have a switch I turn off when things get too intense. But that's something Maggie hasn't had to learn. She's an important person to me, Mike, and I don't want her hurt. Think it over. I'll wait here till I see your car."

"All right, sir," Shayne said wearily.

Hitchcock's tone sharpened. "Stop calling me sir."

Shayne found his Ford and drove it back to the entrance of the little alley. He blinked his lights at Hitchcock's Lincoln, which pulled out and passed him. Hitchcock crouched forward, as though over the wheel of a low-slung racer. He was surprisingly aggressive in traffic, and Shayne had a hard time keeping him in sight. They were somewhere in Georgetown, he knew, but he couldn't keep track of the turns. In Q Street, the Senator braked to a violent stop alongside a brick wall. Shayne slid the Ford in behind him.

Hitchcock met him on the sidewalk. "Before I start shouting at my daughter I'd better make sure. I hoped she and Maggie would hit it off, but I know it hasn't worked. Trina has exalted ideas about how senators ought to behave. It's strange, considering the number of senators she knows. I take it she hired you to see to it that Maggie has a headache from now on when I want to take her to supper?"

"I can't answer that," Shayne said. "I admit she threw an ashtray at me, but maybe it had nothing to do with you."

"I doubt it, somehow," Hitchcock said. "Another thing

I've gotten used to is witnesses who stand on the Fifth Amendment and refuse to answer."

He unlocked a door in the wall and stood aside to let Shayne precede him into a small garden, lighted by an antique gas lamppost that had been converted to electricity. The house was built of weathered brick. It was solid and handsome, and looked old. As Hitchcock opened the front door Trina half-ran into the broad hall to meet them.

She gave Shayne a disgusted look, which told Hitchcock what he wanted to know. Then she bore down on her father.

"Daddy, don't fly off the handle! You know what the doctor said about not getting excited."

"I'm holding myself in quite well, wouldn't you say, Mike?" Hitchcock said. "All I want now are the answers to one or two questions, such as why and what weapons did you use against her and who's paying Mike's fee."

"In a minute," she said desperately. "Tom Wall's in the living room."

"That's convenient. Did you arrange it?"

"No! He's being very mysterious, but apparently he's onto something that will really fix Sam Toby's wagon. He wants to report to you before he goes any further. Daddy, please don't be mad. You'll thank me for it eventually. Somebody has to look out for you."

"It's comforting to know I have such a motherly daughter," Hitchcock said bitterly.

A man burst out of the living room, walking fast and jerkily. He was short and thin, seemingly nothing but bone and sinew. He had sharp black eyes, a jaunty little black mustache, and hollowed cheeks.

"Emory! Something important. Do you mind?"

He looked at Shayne, and Hitchcock said mildly, "Michael Shayne, Senator Tom Wall."

Wall acknowledged the introduction with a fast nod. "Time's passing. At least I won't have to chase you around the supperclubs tonight, that's one consolation. This has all the earmarks of something terrific, and I need your OK on it. Remember a jerk named Bixler who used to work for the

42

subcommittee?" He shot Shayne another accusing glance. "We'd better keep this in the family till tomorrow. It's big, Emory."

"Keep calm, Tom," Hitchcock said. "That's what people tell me, and it's good advice. I have a slight family problem, but it can wait. Trina, take Mike into the library and give him a drink. You'll have a chance to synchronize your stories."

The two senators went off, with Hitchcock's hand on the shorter man's shoulder. Trina took Shayne into a comfortable room smelling of cigars and leather. It was lined with bookshelves from the floor to the ceiling. A few logs smouldered in a fireplace. On a long worktable against one wall Shayne saw an antique wooden press, pots of glue, and other bookbinding equipment. After opening a small cabinet and taking out several bottles, Trina saw Shayne examining the press.

"Here's where Daddy really works," she said. "The Senate's only a hobby. Wasn't cognac what you were drinking on the fishing boat this morning? Shall I get some ice?"

"Straight's fine."

She splashed some cognac into a large snifter and poured herself a half-glass of Cointreau.

"Damn it!" she said with suppressed fury. "I hoped he wouldn't have to know anything about this. Now I'm in the doghouse for fair, not that I really mind so long as that creature is taken care of. What went wrong?"

Shayne took the glass. "You said he was picking her up after the theatre and I thought I had plenty of time. He walked in on us. I'd just taken a gun away from her, and for a few minutes we were all of us breathing hard."

"A gun!"

"She wasn't going to shoot me unless she had to. It was just to make me hold still so she could slug me with an ashtray. She wanted him to hear her version before ours. She broke her date with him for tonight and she told him she's thinking of going to New York tomorrow. Where do we go from here?"

Trina bit her lip and sat down on a leather sofa, tucking her feet beneath her. Shayne sampled the brandy and let her adjust. The brandy was excellent.

"Naturally I wish it hadn't happened this way," she said. "It's going to look like a bad case of interference on my part, and I don't know what I'm going to say."

"Would you like to hear my opinion?" Shayne said.

"Of course."

"I think we'll have to tell him the whole thing. He knows I hit her with something, and he'll want to know what. I can keep on not talking, but I'll be going home tomorrow. You have to go on living with him."

"Oh God. You're right, I suppose. But *you* tell him, Mike —I couldn't. And just watch! She'll wriggle out of it. He's an imbecile as far as that woman's concerned. He'll forgive her! You liked her, didn't you?"

"I like lots of people," Shayne said, looking at his cognac.

"That's not what I meant. You thought she was very strong sexy stuff and you can understand how Daddy feels."

Shayne decided it was time to change the subject. "What's this business with Senator Wall?"

"Oh, he's the number-two man on the subcommittee. This investigation would have never got off the ground if it had not been for Tom. He's a great believer in honesty in government, to the degree that I'm afraid he gets under people's skin." She added hastily, "By that I don't mean that Daddy *doesn't* believe in honesty in government. He just isn't a fanatic about it. After his heart attack he can't afford to be fanatical about anything."

"Is Bixler trying to sell Wall the same thing he sold me?"

"No, I don't think so, not from the way Tom talked about it. He kept saying it would blow the whole case sky-high. Well, maybe. Meanwhile, don't you think we have to assume that the status quo still exists? That Daddy's still their major target?"

She tasted her Cointreau and licked the taste off her lips. "What worries me—as soon as they hear that the Maggie Smith thing has fallen through, won't they try some desperate last-minute move? What I'm getting at, couldn't you stand by, as a sort of bodyguard, for twenty-four hours?"

"Not unless your father agrees."

"Well, he wouldn't agree. But couldn't you watch him without letting him realize you were there?"

Shayne shook his head. "That only happens in books, Miss Hitchcock. I'm a stranger in town. And even if I'd worked here all my life, I'd need three other men and a couple of two-way radios, and I wouldn't guarantee anything."

She worried her lip for another minute. "But at least you'll make sure Maggie Smith gets on a plane tomorrow? And if anything comes up before then, where will you be?"

"At the St. Albans," Shayne told her, without adding that after he got to sleep it would take more than the ringing of the telephone to wake him up.

Hitchcock came in.

"Tom's wonderful," he said to his daughter, his usual good temper restored. "He's going to be majority leader in ten years, or dead of a heart attack." He knocked lightly on the desk top. "Knock on wood."

"Don't joke about it!" Trina said harshly. "It's in terrible taste."

"I had some mild heart trouble a while ago," the Senator explained to Shayne. "I recommend it as a good way to get a sensible outlook. Trina, I'll get around to you shortly. I want to talk to Mike privately first. Don't go to bed."

She stood up. "Daddy, I'm sorry."

"I know you are, dear, and I hope not too much damage has been done."

She smiled nervously and left them alone.

CHAPTER 6

10:05 P.M.

HITCHCOCK POURED MORE BRANDY INTO SHAYNE'S GLASS AND set the bottle beside his chair. "Help yourself when you feel like it. I have to deny myself hard liquor, but they've relented about cigars. Without cigars, I think I might have had to resign from the Senate. Will you smoke one with me? These are Havanas. I wish I could think they were part of a pre-Castro shipment. Actually, I know very well that they were smuggled in."

As soon as their cigars were burning evenly, Hitchcock said, "Perhaps I should explain about my daughter. Her mother was an invalid for many years before she died. I was away much of the time, first in the legislature, then in Washington. Even after they joined me here we didn't have much family life. She's concerned about me. In my turn I'm concerned about her. I have a strong hunch that she and Tom Wall are having an affair. There's nothing wrong with Tom except that he eats ravenously and never puts on weight. He's too eager for my taste, and besides that he's married. His wife isn't here with him, but it worries me. Well, that's neither here nor there. I'm already talking too much, but that's a habit we find it easy to fall into. Maggie —ever since she was a young girl she's been part of the theatre, and I don't have to be told that few theatrical people live by traditional American small-town standards. Although some of the things that go on in American small towns! I know there have been men in her life. That has nothing to do with my feeling for her."

He waited for some comment from Shayne, drawing on his long Havana, but the detective kept quiet.

"Our friendship has been entirely platonic," Hitchcock said. "I wouldn't expect Trina to believe that. I think what frightens her is the possibility that I might marry again. What frightens *me* is what Maggie would say if I asked her. Well, I know she'd be kind. I can't seem to stop talking about her. She's so *alive!* You saw that, didn't you?"

Shayne nodded slowly, having no trouble remembering the way Maggie Smith had felt in his arms.

"What has your investigation turned up about her?" Hitchcock asked, too casually. "I really think you'd better tell me, Mike. Otherwise I'll have to squeeze it out of Trina, which would be unpleasant for both of us. If you can drive Maggie out of town with it, it must be fairly lurid."

Shayne swirled the brandy around in the big bubble of glass. "I hate to do it this way, Senator. She did something for Sam Toby once. I can give you the details if you have to have them, but I'd just as soon leave it at that. She didn't deny it."

Hitchcock's face had gone very still. "When?"

"Eight years ago. I know people change, and I think she's sorry. But it raises a big question. Apparently she's pretty close to the rocks financially. You know this guy Sam Toby and the way he operates. Leaving personalities aside, do you think he's capable of putting a hustler on you?"

"Toby is capable of anything if there's enough money involved and he thinks he can get away with it." He laid his cigar carefully in an ashtray and stood up. "Excuse me."

With his back turned, he poured a glass of water from a carafe on the worktable and swallowed two pills that he took from a small vial. Shayne was on his feet.

"Is there anything I can do, Senator?"

"No. This is precautionary."

After a moment he turned, went to the phone on a small table beside the fireplace, and began to dial.

Shayne said, "Why not sleep on it? Let her call you."

"Do you think I'd sleep?"

He waited. The phone rang a long time. Then Shayne heard the connection being opened and Hitchcock said quietly, "Maggie?"

There was a faint scratching noise. Hitchcock turned up

a volume control and reached over to throw a switch so the conversation would be recorded.

Maggie Smith's voice said, "—feel much better. The Senate ought to put up a statue to the man who invented aspirin. But about tomorrow. A call came through from New York just after you left. I have to run up to untangle a stupid legal snafu about some out-of-town performance rights. It's too boring to go into. I may not be back for several days."

"I have Mike Shayne here," Hitchcock said. "I've been browbeating him. Naturally I couldn't believe that he'd been interviewing you about some runaway hoodlum. There was too much excitement in the air."

"What has he told you?"

"Not much as yet, except that he was able to scare you with some scandal he dredged up out of the past. Ordinarily I'd refuse to listen, but in anything involving Sam Toby you must realize that I have a public responsibility. I can't leave it hanging in midair."

"Don't tell me Shayne won't supply the details. I wouldn't give him credit for so much delicacy."

"I'd rather hear it from you, if you don't mind."

She sighed. "I've always known it would come back to haunt me. I've dreamed about it, except that in my dreams it turned into a murder and I couldn't get rid of the body. You've been sweet, Emory. I'll say goodbye to you now, because I know you won't be speaking to me in another minute."

"Don't be too sure," Hitchcock said softly.

"Emory—" She waited a moment, and Shayne could guess that her eyes were shut and she was pinching the bridge of her nose. She said it fast. "I wanted a part in a Broadway production. My thirtieth birthday was coming up, and it seemed to me that that was some kind of deadline. I had to find out if I was really an actress before it was too late. Sam was never a real friend of mine, but I've known him a long time. He knew people who were putting up the money for a show with a second lead that was right for me. Emory, you do know that in the theatre it's not exactly unheard of for an actress to go to bed with a producer to get a part she wants very much?"

Hitchcock kept his voice noncommittal; Shayne, in the same room with him, could see what it cost. "Yes, I've heard of that happening."

"It's part of the folklore," she said bitterly. "So Sam arranged it. It's the sort of thing he does well. I was promised the part if I would invest a week or so in a Caribbean cruise with a Labor Department official. I'd just had my divorce and it was a rough one. I didn't like anybody very much, including myself. Sam introduced me to the man. He seemed quite ordinary and inoffensive. Sam's client needed an exemption from the Wage-Hour Act for a certain category of workers, as I understood it. I know it was a lousy thing to do, and I've been regretting it steadily ever since. I went on the cruise, and I actually had a fairly good time. Sam's client was given the exemption. I got the part, and the play folded after three days. I was OK in it, but not wonderful, I guess. Producers didn't embarrass me with floods of offers."

"Thank you for being so frank," Hitchcock said without expression.

"That was the first and only time anything like that happened. Sam never mentioned it again. In the last few years I've hardly seen him. Mike Shayne says that Sam made the arrangements so I could meet you. This was news to me. I can see how under the circumstances you won't believe that. I've been puzzling and puzzling. Maybe Sam's holding me in reserve or something, but I don't know. If he has anything up his sleeve, why hasn't he mentioned it to me?"

She didn't bother to make it sound convincing. "I know you've absorbed all the implications by now," she went on. "In the face of this much evidence, what can I hope to gain by denying it? But I do, Emory. I haven't been spying on you. I haven't planned this with Sam Toby. I'm not scheming to get you into a motel bed in front of a camera, as Shayne thinks. And now I really do have a headache. I feel lousy in other ways too."

"What are we going to do?" Hitchcock said in a strangled voice.

Maggie seemed to be close to total exhaustion. "Do? We aren't going to see each other any more. That's obvious. Michael Shayne will pocket his fee and go home. Don't worry about it, Emory. It isn't that important."

They both waited with the line open, but there was nothing else either of them wanted to say.

"Goodbye, Maggie, I'm sorry," Hitchcock said finally, and put back the phone.

He worked slowly at his cigar while Shayne finished his brandy in silence. Suddenly Hitchcock hammered his fist against his knee.

"I believe her! Good God, I've done things I'm ashamed of, we all have. I'm sorry she got mixed up in that old affair with Toby, but we wouldn't ever learn anything if we didn't make mistakes. I don't care—she *couldn't* have been pretending these last two months."

"She's an actress," Shayne pointed out. "Most of the love scenes in the movies look like the real thing."

"No, Mike. You met her for the first time tonight." He stared at the ash on his cigar. "I've had conversations with her lasting for hours. Some of the things she's said—a fake? They couldn't have been! I expect you'll think I've gone into my second childhood, but damn it—"

All this proved, of course, was that Maggie Smith had been good in the role, which Shayne had been sure of already.

"She said something about Toby arranging for us to meet," Hitchcock said. "What did she mean?"

"Mrs. Redpath asked you to dinner as a favor for Toby. She told me that herself."

"Adelle?" Hitchcock frowned, puzzled. "If she says so I'll have to accept it, but that doesn't prove Maggie was in on it."

"It's a good indication." Looking down into his glass, Shayne picked his arguments carefully. "Even if you're not entirely convinced, won't you want to call time until the

50

hearings are over? If Maggie's telling the truth she'll understand why you can't afford to take any chances."

The Senator shook his head slowly. "You're advising me to withhold judgment. But that's not how it would look to her. She'd think I'd convicted her without giving her any real chance to explain. Damn it, I shouldn't have been as cold as that on the phone. I hate to think what she must be going through right now."

"She didn't admit that Caribbean cruise until she had to," Shayne pointed out.

Hitchcock went on as though the detective hadn't spoken. "In a strange way, this is my last chance, Mike. The last chance I may ever have to get hold of anything real. I can't let it end like this."

"Why the hell not?" Shayne exclaimed, suddenly losing his patience with the stubborn old man. "Your daughter will tell you that she didn't have an easy time getting me up here. I agreed to come because I didn't like the idea of someone in your position being played for a patsy in what looks like an up-to-date version of the old badger game. OK—maybe it's not, but it sure as hell looks like it, and why not play safe for a couple of weeks?"

"Because Maggie isn't an abstraction, Mike. She's a person."

"Oh, my God! Well, there's an old rule among con-men— the victim has to be willing. If you think you absolutely have to talk to her tomorrow, will you let me fix the place, and go over it first for bugs and cameras?"

"No, Mike. Either I trust her or I don't."

Shayne put the glass beside the bottle. Sitting forward, he planted his big hands on his knees.

"Your daughter told me this wouldn't take more than a couple of hours. I didn't really expect it to be that simple. Before I go, Senator, would you mind telling me a few things that have no connection with Maggie Smith? What did Senator Redpath have to do with awarding this contract?"

"Redpath?" Hitchcock said, surprised. "You're asking because of Adelle's dinner, of course, and that's hardly unconnected with Maggie Smith. You're giving this too much weight, Mike. We could have met in any of dozens of ways." He considered, drawing on his cigar. "Hank Redpath—well, I wonder. Half the Senate was involved with the contract on one side or the other. How much do you know about it?"

"Very damn little. I know who won, and that's about all."

"Who lost is more important. National Aviation isn't accustomed to losing contracts of this size. They're a big amalgamation of a half-dozen companies, and their political connections, their military connections, their banking connections are all very good. They make a point of spotting their subcontracts in swing states where there are senators who expect a hard fight for reelection and are looking for campaign contributions. That's where the real lobbying takes place, back in the states. It's one reason our investigations here never do more than scratch the surface. Is this the kind of thing you want?"

"More or less."

"Manners Aerosystems also has plants in a number of states, but it's mainly a Texas company. As you may know, the Texas delegation pulls a disproportionate amount of weight in this town. But they couldn't have done it alone. Redpath would be a good ally. He has twelve years' seniority on the Finance Committee, where the brass hats have to come every year for money. If Redpath had a strong opinion on the merits of one contender versus the other, unquestionably he would have been listened to. But sooner or later most cloakroom rumors end up with me, and I haven't heard this one. Oh, he may have made a few phone calls and written a few routine letters."

Hitchcock's eyes were wandering. He couldn't seem to keep his mind on what he was saying. He said suddenly, "Here's an idea. I recorded that phone conversation with Maggie. Why don't I spring that on Toby? Tell him to stop putting pressure on her or I'll give it to the papers. There's no statute of limitations on publicity. I couldn't put him in jail with it, but I could hurt him."

Shayne stood up. "Leave blackmail to the experts, Senator. You could hurt Toby but you'd also hurt Maggie. He'd think it over and tell you to go ahead."

Hitchcock's face fell. "You're right, of course."

"I don't suppose you want to tell me what Senator Wall is so hopped up about?"

"Tom Wall gets hopped up faster and more easily than any other man in the Senate. And sometimes for less cause."

Shayne pulled at his earlobe indecisively. "That does it, then. I can't think of anything else."

Hitchcock came to the door with him. "Mike, I keep thinking of reasons I ought to believe her. Toby must know I couldn't drop the investigation at this stage even if I wanted to. After it gets to public hearings, it picks up it own momentum. It's really been Tom's baby, anyway. Why not pick on him? And rumors aside, giving the contract to Manners was the proper thing to do. He was well in the lead on performance points. He's one of the few industrial geniuses still around. The time for an investigation would have been if National had got it." His mind skipped back to Maggie. "Just because I haven't promised not to see her again, don't make that an excuse to hector her any more, Mike. I mean that."

"I've done everything I can with the facts I have," Shayne said. "You're over twenty-one."

"I'm glad somebody around here realizes that. You look tired. Go to bed and stop worrying. I can take care of myself."

Shayne said goodnight soberly. He intended to go to bed, because he didn't know what else to do, but he didn't expect to stop worrying. Could Senator Hitchcock take care of himself? From what Shayne had seen so far, he doubted it very much.

CHAPTER 7
10:25 P.M.

THE SAVAGE GROOVES AROUND MICHAEL SHAYNE'S EYES AND mouth were deeply etched as he came out of Senator Hitchcock's house on Q Street. If Senator Wall had turned up something that could damage Sam Toby or the Texas crowd in the next day's hearing, they couldn't be expected to stand still and wait for it to happen. Their Maggie Smith gambit had failed, for the time being. But no professional—and Sam Toby was clearly that—stays at the top of his league without developing an assortment of pitches. He had missed with his fast ball, and now he'd come in with his curve or his slider. More than ever, Shayne was aware of not knowing the rules of the game he was playing.

He hesitated before getting into his Ford. And in that half-second a flicker of movement a block away pulled at his eye.

A man stepped out of a parked car and started in his direction. Shayne's years of living with danger had given him a kind of built-in warning system, and all the bells were clanging violently. He waited. The sidewalk was deserted except for the approaching stranger. He was built like a light heavyweight. He walked with a swing, on the balls of his feet.

In front of Senator Hitchcock's house, Shayne decided, was the wrong place for trouble. He lit a cigarette unhurriedly and slid behind the wheel. Swinging the rearview mirror, he picked up the approaching figure. The man quickened his step, then slowed abruptly as Shayne put the Ford in gear and moved away. A heavy car left the line of parked cars behind him. It looked like a Buick, the largest model in the most expensive series. Picking up the man on the sidewalk, it followed Shayne's Ford, accelerating.

Shayne still didn't hurry. He waited till the other car was close enough so he could see that it carried Texas plates. Then he came down hard on the gas and shot away.

There was a slight grin on his lips and much of the tension had left his face. So far he had been groping his way blindfolded through an enemy minefield, knowing that the only safe thing to do was nothing at all. This was something he knew how to handle. These men were amateurs. If they had wanted to find out where he went, they should have stayed out of sight. If they had wanted to pick him up, they should have jumped him the minute he came out of the house.

He inched across each major intersection, making a big point of looking at street signs. The Texans too were in a strange town, and he didn't want them to lose him before he found out more about them. He swung into one of the city's numerous traffic circles, holding his speed at 35. A statue of a general on horseback drifted by on his left. Having passed that same statue several times, he knew where he was: in Sheridan Circle. There was a dazzle of headlights in his mirror. He didn't bother to sort them out; if they lost him at this speed they weren't worth worrying about. He was looking for the right kind of bar, and found it after turning onto Wisconsin Avenue—a small place called the Bijou, with a doorman and a marquee.

He parked on a side street. Walking back he staggered slightly, as though the cognac was finally beginning to take over. He stumbled, caught himself quickly and wished the Bijou doorman a pleasant good evening. The doorman gave him a suspicious look in return, but decided that he wasn't quite drunk enough yet to be refused admittance. Out of the corner of his eye, Shayne saw the Buick coast past. As well as he could judge, there was only one man in the front seat besides the driver.

Inside, he had a choice between sitting at the bar or going on into a poorly-lighted room to listen to a woman with a ravaged face singing Cole Porter songs, leaning against the curve of a grand piano. She hadn't attracted much of a crowd. The headwaiter tried to steer Shayne in to a table, where he would be subject to a cover charge. Shayne waved him away. Reaching out, he caught the rim of the bar and pulled himself in against it. He grinned at the bartender.

"I see a bottle of Martell's on the back bar. That shows good taste on somebody's part. In a wine glass, and I'll have a glass of ice water with it."

He swung onto a high stool at the heel of the bar, from which he could watch the new arrivals. There weren't many. Leaning on both elbows, he rested. They knew where he was. They had to come to him.

He heard a spattering of applause in the other room, and the singer gave her small audience an ironic bow and walked off, leaving the pianist to continue without her.

A short way down the bar, two men were arguing drunkenly about Sam Toby. Probably, Shayne thought, this was the main subject all over Washington tonight. One of the men was sure that Toby would beat this rap, as he had beaten all the others over the years. He had half the Senate membership in his pocket, because he knew their weaknesses. And Hugh Manners—there was a *man*. Why didn't the goddamn politicians leave him alone? What if he did have to bribe a few people so they'd let him stay in the competition? The other drinker maintained that Toby's days were numbered. Why would they call him to testify unless they had something on him? Shayne, too, would like to know the answer to that question, among others, but he did not think he would get it here.

A plump, fair-haired man in a black silk suit came in from the street with a blonde girl. They were bickering quietly, like husband and wife. He went on into the main room and the girl came over to the bar, where she took a stool once removed from Shayne and ordered crème de menthe. She kept looking at her watch impatiently. She lit a cigarette, which she took from a silver case in a small evening bag, and put it out again after a few puffs. When the man didn't return, Shayne gave her a closer look.

She was in her early twenties. Most of the things that had happened to her so far had obviously been pleasant. Her features were finely cut, with a shadow of dissatisfaction at the corners of her mouth. Her white dress had a short skirt, very little back, and not much front. She wore a diamond necklace that looked authentic to Shayne. He didn't know much about diamonds but he was an expert on girls, and he knew that this one couldn't be picked up in this kind of bar unless she had been told to by someone with money to spend. So he decided to try.

He swayed in her direction. "People all told me back home that Washington's a dead town after dark. *Dead?* It's putrid."

She glanced at him coolly, moved her drink a fraction of an inch farther away and went on looking at her watch. But she stayed where she was, though there were half a dozen empty stools farther down.

"You didn't have the privilege of hearing the singer," Shayne said loosely. "That was an experience. She got up off her deathbed to fill the engagement. Fascinating, if you like ghoulish entertainment. One number there, 'Night and Day,' I was giving three to one she wouldn't make it all the way through. Rallied in the middle. What's that in your glass?"

"Crème de menthe," she said indifferently.

"Crème de *what?*" he said, almost falling off his stool. "Never heard of it. What's it taste like?"

Without asking her permission he lurched closer, picked the glass out of her hands and tasted it. He recoiled.

"Say, that's horrible! That's the worst drink I ever tasted. I'd rather take cough syrup. Let me buy you something that will stir up your circulation. You're a good-looking kid except for one thing—you're too pale."

"Thanks," she said with another look at her watch. "I'll stick with this."

"Baby, don't you know when your date has run out on you?" Shayne said. "Or hasn't it ever happened to you before? He's been gone fifteen minutes. What did he tell you? He was going to the men's room? Don't believe it. He left by the back door."

She frowned. "Why would he do that?"

"I could name you any number of reasons. I'm more or less in the business myself. Maybe there's somebody in there he didn't want to see you together. He's a married man, right?"

She looked at Shayne fully for the first time. "His wife is in California. Listen, would you be willing to—"

She stopped, frowning again.

"To check the men's room for you?" Shayne said happily. "Baby, I will do that with the greatest of pleasure."

He straightened his shoulders. Coming down too hard on his heels, he walked a straight line to the men's room, where there was a colored attendant but no customers. Checking his appearance in the mirror, Shayne rumpled his hair and loosened the knot of his tie. His eyes were already bloodshot, from a shortage of sleep, not from too much liquor.

"Nobody there but us chickens," he reported to the girl after returning to the bar. "Bartender! Make mine a double this time, and for the lady—" He looked at her. "Not that goo, for God's sake."

"What are you having?"

"Martell's. The best cognac you can get in a creep joint like this."

He waved at the bartender. When the drinks came he attacked his thirstily, spilling part of it. The girl didn't like this, but Shayne no longer doubted that she was following orders.

"Honey, we've got to get out of here," he told her earnestly. "I'm beginning to feel like a mummy, and that's not what good cognac is supposed to do for you. That singer's going to come back any minute. There has to be *one* livelier place than this in town." He tightened his necktie and said, "Michael Shayne, from Miami, Florida, the greatest little city in the world. I can tell just from looking at you—" he looked at her solemnly "—that you don't ordinarily take drinks from strangers in bars. But this is an emergency! Washington's reputation is at stake! You don't want me to die of boredom, do you? How would that look in the papers?"

He clutched at his chest suddenly and staggered, his face going blank. She clapped her hand to her mouth and her eyes widened. Shayne was being watched closely by the bartender and the headwaiter. He laughed.

"Relax, everybody. I'm in excellent health. Only clowning. I just mean," he said to the girl, "it's your duty, and if you have any stublic pirit at all—"

He looked doubtful. "What did I say? That didn't sound right."

She gave him a grudging smile, showing excellent teeth. "I think you said if I had any public pirit."

"I'm not drunk," Shayne assured her. "I'm not exactly stone-cold sober either, but I want you to know that I'm hitting on all cylinders. What kind of nice first name do you have?"

"Cheryl," she murmured.

"Cheryl! Did you hear that, bartender? Cheryl happens to be one of my favorite girl's names. What do you say, Cheryl, are we getting out of here?"

She studied him, smiling faintly. "I suppose if it's my duty. I do know a place with a very gaudy nude floor show."

"Well, now," Shayne said. "I'm not one of those people who slobber every time they see a female nude, but I've got nothing against them. What are we killing time here for?"

He finished his drink. She wasn't drinking fast enough to suit him so he took her glass out of her hands and finished it for her. The headwaiter was hovering nearby, in case he needed help making the door. Shayne brushed him out of his way and headed for the street in a stiff careful walk. The girl followed.

Outside in the darkness, he wavered from the curb in to the storefronts and back.

"This town!" he said in disgust. "With all the taxes we pay they can't even get the sidewalks to stay level."

Cheryl, laughing, hugged his arm. He dragged her toward his Ford, continuing to weave and wobble while he examined both sides of the dark street. He spotted a motionless figure in a doorway across from his car. There would be one other somewhere. Shayne didn't think this would be considered more than a two-man job.

He wrapped his arms around the girl and attempted to kiss her. But Cheryl didn't want to lose status by being kissed on a public sidewalk, and while they were pushing and tugging at each other Shayne lurched against his car and located the second man, crouched on the floor behind the front seat, his face hidden.

"Baby, you're gorgeous," Shayne said with enthusiasm. "You're the nicest thing that's happened to me in months."

"Mike, behave yourself."

"What's wrong with the way I'm behaving? Are you implying I'm not being respectful?"

"Of course not." She gave his waist a squeeze. "You keep in good shape, don't you?"

"I try to," Shayne said modestly. "But I don't get enough sleep. Too damn much else to do. You know what I like about you? The way you carry yourself. It's the one essential thing I insist on in a dame. Instead of going someplace hot and stuffy, what we could do, let's get in the back seat and stretch out."

She jerked his hand away from the door handle. "No!"

"If you don't want to, OK," Shayne said, aggrieved, "but I didn't like the way you said that."

"I need a couple of drinks first. You're way ahead of me. I only just met you! Afterwards, if all goes well—" Reaching up with both hands, she pulled his head down, gave him a quick businesslike kiss and whispered, "But not now, darling."

Having disposed of that problem, she said briskly, "Get in this side. I'll drive."

Shayne said dangerously, reeling away, "Are you trying to tell me I'm in no condition to drive? I'm the best driver you'll ever see, drunk *or* sober."

Reeling back, he opened the front door for her and put her in. On his way to the driver's side, he misjudged the curb and fell down. He was up again at once, grinning.

"They build some tricky sidewalks up here, don't they?"

He slid behind the wheel and toppled over on her. "You and me are going to have a wonderful time." Seizing her, he kissed her hard. He hadn't liked the businesslike kiss she had doled out to him, and he made this a real one, keeping his eyes open for any signs of life from the back seat. After a moment he felt her respond. She gasped when he let her go.

"Mike—Jesus—"

"What did I tell you?" Shayne said. "I knew you were a swinger."

He swayed back to his own side of the seat, snapped on the ignition and started the motor, his head still turned toward her. Her eyes wavered.

The man behind them didn't think he had to be careful. Cheryl seized Shayne's arm and cried, pointing out through the windshield, "Mike, *what's that?*"

He delayed a fraction of a second until his assailant had committed himself to his swing, then thrust the girl away and came up fast, catching the man's forearm. He jerked it forward and brought it down hard on the steering wheel. He had the wrist in one hand, the elbow in the other, and gave it an extra twist at the moment of impact. He heard the bone break.

The blackjack fell limply between Shayne and the girl. She screamed, sounding more surprised than frightened. Shayne rammed the automatic transmission into drive and stamped on the gas.

The second man across the street had left the doorway of the apartment house where he had been waiting. Shayne swung the wheel and headed straight at him, his headlights on full. As Shayne had expected, it was the plump man with the long hair, who had come into the Bijou with Cheryl. The headlights blinded him. He halted, crouching, then darted to one side. Grinning wolfishly, his foot all the way down, Shayne went up on the sidewalk after him. The man whirled. His face had gone dead white. He shouted something, both hands up to ward off the Ford, and leaped into the doorway.

Shayne hit the brakes. The Ford skidded to a stop with its front bumper sealing the doorway. The man scrabbled frantically at the locked door of the apartment lobby. Shayne threw the transmission into neutral, snatched the blackjack off the floor and was out of the car in one swift fluid motion. He vaulted onto the hood, the blackjack ready, The man's body contracted as he looked over his shoulder at the powerfully-built redhead above him.

Cheryl was trying to move the injured thug so she could reach the wheel. Shayne said with quiet authority, "Better not, Cheryl. You only had one chance. Nothing you can do about it now."

The man with the broken arm had begun to feel sorry for himself as the pain reached him. Cheryl went on pulling at him. "Damn you, Morrie, get out of the way."

Shayne said more sharply, "Don't you know when something's gone sour? Cut it out or we'll have a few broken skulls." He motioned to the frightened man in the doorway. "Climb over. Don't hurry. We have lots of time."

The man made an effort to recover his composure. Ordinarily his plump cheeks probably gave him a self-satisfied look. He smoothed his hair, gave it a final pat on each side, and stepped up on the bumper.

"You seem to be under the impression—"

Shayne slapped the blackjack smartly against his palm. "I'm not the one who made the mistake."

"Curt," the girl called urgently.

But the plump man hadn't recovered from the effects of being pinned against the door by Shayne's Ford. His head was trembling up and down, as though he consented in advance to anything Shayne wanted of him. He slithered across the hood. Shayne patted him under the arms and on the pockets. This was the executive; he wasn't carrying a weapon.

There was movement in the front seat. The man the girl had called Morrie was trying to get his gun out with his left hand. The shoulder holster was one of those with a safety clasp, strapped on at an angle so the gun would resist a pull from anyone but its rightful owner. Shayne reached through the window and slapped him on the temple with the blackjack. He sagged forward against the wheel.

"Where's the Buick?"

Curt glanced along the street. "Let's talk about this," he said in a strained voice.

"Why should I talk to you when I can talk to your boss?"

"I can make you a good offer. Violence won't get us anywhere."

"What made you change your mind?" Shayne signaled to the girl. "Get out, Cheryl. And don't try to run. I think I could catch you, but I'd have to blackjack your friend here first."

"He's no friend of mine," she said coldly. She opened the door and came around the car. "I'll say somebody made a mistake. That was a pretty good drunk act. The only thing wrong was that kiss."

"I didn't have my mind on it, Cheryl," Shayne said, opening the Ford's front door.

"Well, sometime when you're able to give it your undivided attention—"

Shayne worked the unconscious gunman into position so he could pull his fangs. The gun was a short-barreled .38. Shayne dropped it into his side pocket.

"I wish I could trust somebody to get the Buick," he said, "but for some reason I don't think I can. You two are going to have to carry him. Be careful of his arm. You don't want to compound that fracture."

Curt looked in at the limp figure. "He must weigh about one-ninety. I don't think we can."

"Try," Shayne suggested.

Curt pulled the injured man to the edge of the seat. He returned to consciousness suddenly with a long moan.

"Does it hurt?" Curt said without sympathy. "It wouldn't have happened if you'd been quicker with the sap, would it? We're going for a short walk, Shayne tells us. Cooperate."

Morrie protested, making a cradle of his left arm to support his broken right. Curt wrestled him out of the door and then Shayne moved the Ford back to the street and parked parallel to the curb. Curt and the girl walked Morrie toward the Buick, all three huddled together with the gunman whimpering between them.

Reaching the bigger car, Curt opened the back door and Morrie fell in on the floor.

"Don't pass out yet," the redhead said. "I want to see what else you've got in your pockets."

Morrie rolled on one hip, and Shayne took a thick wallet from his buttoned back pocket. There was nothing of interest in the other pockets except a half-dozen loose rounds for the .38. Shayne took those, while Morrie groaned and pleaded for a doctor.

"Nobody ever died of a broken arm," Shayne said. "You're next, Curt."

"Seriously," Curt said. "He wasn't supposed to chill you, just tap you so you'd sit quiet and listen."

"But he got carried away," Shayne said.

"The man's a moron, but he's the best I could do on short notice. I want to persuade you to go back to Miami, Shayne. Tell me how much they're paying you and I'll double it."

A car went by without slackening speed.

"You don't want cops," Shayne said, "and neither do I, so let's see how fast we can mop this up. Dump everything out on the hood."

"Shayne—"

"Will you shut up? I'm tired."

He stuck the blackjack in his belt and began looking through their wallets. Curt, he found, was carrying over two thousand dollars in large bills. His last name was Rebman, and his address in the identification window was a hotel in Houston, Texas. In case of an accident, such as the one he was now having, notification was to be made to the Manners Aerosystems Co. Morrie, on the other hand, wanted his mother notified; she too lived in Houston.

"You'll need it in cash," Curt said, refusing to believe that he couldn't reach Shayne if he named a large enough figure. "Take what I've got there as a down payment. Another two or three thousand would be no problem at all. And all you have to do to earn it is get on a plane."

"Where would you get that much cash at this time of night?"

"I said it wouldn't be a problem."

64

Shayne smiled and took Cheryl's bag out of her hands.

"Oh, no, you don't!" she said, snatching for it.

"Goddamn it! Will you people get it through your head that you're in trouble? I can take you in and charge you with assault. I know you don't worry about gun registrations in Texas, but does Morrie have a permit in Washington? This would break in the morning papers, just before the hearings. Use your head."

He emptied the girl's bag, and in addition to the usual feminine equipment, he found a folded letter addressed to Miss Cheryl Remick, at a Northwest address, and postmarked Houston. Inside there was a single sheet of paper, on which was typed, "Royalton Arms," followed by a 16th Street NW address and that day's date.

"Reading other people's mail," she said.

"I've heard that Manners likes good-looking girls your age," Shayne said. "Is that where he is now, at the Royalton Arms?"

"You can always go there and find out," she said.

"No, Cheryl," Curt said. "Shayne's right, this has gone sour. What do you want to talk to him about, Shayne? I might just tell you where you can find him."

A car with a long aerial approached slowly. Shayne swept up the wallets and the handbag and dropped them into his already bulging pockets. He closed the Buick's back door before the cruising police car reached them, and pulled his coat together to hide the blackjack.

"You don't want to call it a night," he said to the girl. "Let's call up some people. It's my birthday, isn't it? I want to celebrate."

The police car went out of gear as it came abreast. The uniformed cop beside the driver looked them over impassively. Curt smiled at him.

"Evening, officer," he said in a thick Texas accent. "Warm tonight."

"Take it easy," the cop said, chiefly to Shayne.

The redhead grinned. "Little birthday celebration."

The cops went back into gear and proceeded to Wisconsin Avenue, where they joined the southbound traffic.

"He's a hard man to get in to see," Rebman went on, "but I think I can talk him into it. I agree with you, if you're going to be talking money, you might as well talk about it with the man who has it. He expects me to handle things like this without bothering him, but never mind. Let's get going."

"I don't want to be outnumbered when I get there," Shayne said.

He slapped Curt lightly with the blackjack. The Texan made a sick sound and sat down in the street.

"What did you do that for?" the girl cried.

"Because he talks too much," Shayne said. "Are you wearing stockings?" He flicked up her white skirt. "Let's have them."

She didn't move until he said it again. She reached under her skirt to unsnap her garters. Hopping on one foot and then the other, she skinned off the stockings. Shayne used one of them to tie Curt's hands.

"What are you—" Curt said, dazed.

With the other stocking Shayne improvised a gag. Opening the rear door, he tipped Curt in with Morrie.

"Now I'm going to need your slip, if you're wearing one."

"I'm not," Cheryl said.

"That's too bad. Take off your dress."

"This dress cost one hundred and ninety-eight dollars plus sales tax," she said grimly, "and if you think you're going to tear it up, you'll have a fight on your hands."

"I might enjoy it," Shayne said, "but I don't have the time. Make up your mind in a hurry. It can be one of two ways."

He flicked the blackjack hard against the Buick's front fender. The thin steel crumpled.

"You wouldn't hit me with that," she said.

"Take a good look."

She looked into his eyes. "Damn it, Mike," she said after a second. "Why did we have to meet like this? I'd better warn you—I'm not wearing much underneath."

Leaning down, she pulled at the hem of her skirt, trying to tear it. "I'll do that," Shayne said. Cheryl touched his shoulder to keep her balance while he ripped her skirt all the way from the bottom hem to the waist. He tore out a long panel, tore that into strips and bound Curt's ankles. After that he bound and gagged Morrie and turned to the girl.

"I don't suppose you'll make an exception," she said.

"Why should I?"

She stood quietly while he tore off more pieces of her skirt and tied her wrists and ankles. "I'm sorry about that dumb trick in the bar," she said. "I told Hugh I didn't want to do it, but he said I had to. Am I going to see you again?"

"I hope not."

He placed the gag and fastened it, then put her into the back seat with the others.

"My advice," he said, addressing everyone who was still conscious, "is to keep your heads down and try not to move. If anybody calls the cops, you'll get your picture in the paper. Manners won't like that. I'll tell him where he can find you. Just be patient."

He cranked up the windows and went back to his Ford. As he drove past the Buick he tapped his horn.

CHAPTER 8
1:10 A.M.

THE ROYALTON ARMS, A SHABBY BRICK APARTMENT HOUSE in an out-of-the-way neighborhood, seemed an unlikely place to find Hugh Manners. Probably, Shayne decided, the industrialist didn't want the public to know that he was sufficiently worried by the Hitchcock investigation to come to Washington to take personal charge of the counteroffensive.

Shayne reviewed quickly the few things he knew about Manners. Before World War II, Manners' fighter planes had been the fastest in the world. He tested them himself. He had grown up during the glamorous early days of aviation, and he had an obsession with speed. He had walked away from a dozen serious crashes. He ran his company the way he flew his planes—as enormous as it had become in recent years, it was still a one-man business, the last in the industry. His business methods were unorthodox and sometimes brilliant. One year he might make one hundred million dollars, and the next year be in serious danger of losing his shirt. He never gave interviews, believing that his private life was nobody's business. Nevertheless, he had often been in the headlines with spectacular paternity and alimony suits.

There were twelve apartments in the building. Manners' name didn't appear beside the doorbells in the cramped, poorly lit lobby. Curt Rebman was listed as the tenant of a third-floor apartment. Shayne pressed that bell and waited.

There was no answering buzz. Before long he heard footsteps and the door opened. A large man stepped out all the way, closing the door behind him. He was easily six feet six, with the chest-spread of a steer and the relaxed expression of many powerful men. He had been hit in the face various times over the years, by various things that were harder than fists. His eyes were quick and intelligent.

"Michael Shayne to see Mr. Manners," Shayne said.

The big man looked puzzled. "You rang 3-B. Nobody there by that name."

"Curt sent me," Shayne said. "You can give Manners this."

Inside the last piece of Cheryl's skirt, the redhead had tied all the trophies he had taken from her little party: the two wallets, her evening bag, the blackjack, the .38, the loose rounds of ammunition. It made an odd-looking bundle. The big man's eyebrows disappeared in the scar tissue on his forehead. But as he felt the hard outlines of the gun through the cloth, the eyebrows came down in a frown.

"I hope you're not trying to be funny."

"Doesn't Manners have a sense of humor?"

"He hasn't cracked a smile in years. Wait here."

He unlocked the door and went in, and was back again in almost exactly the length of time it would have taken him to go up and down two flights of stairs.

"You get in," he said more pleasantly. "Now don't take this wrong, but I've got to frisk you. That's the condition."

"I'm carrying a fountain pen," Shayne said, "and it's only fair to tell you that it's loaded."

"Will you stop trying to be smart, for your own good?" He extended both his hands toward Shayne's chest. "OK?"

Shayne spread his arms and let the big man go over him rapidly. He was asked to pull up his pants to show that he wasn't carrying a knife or a small gun strapped to his calf. He did so, after which the door was finally opened for him. The big man stayed a half-step behind him going up the stairs.

"What was all that stuff wrapped in? Was that the dress the kid had on?"

"Part of it," Shayne said.

"That's what I thought. Boy, oh boy. This is something I want to see."

On the third floor he let Shayne into a short foyer leading

to a small living room. There was no rug on the floor and not much furniture. What there was looked as though it had been bought from a secondhand dealer by somebody who wasn't concerned about anything but the price. Manners, in his shirt-sleeves and wearing a green eyeshade, was sitting in a swivel chair behind an unpainted kitchen table. There was a neat stack of manila folders in front of him, a phone, an overflowing ashtray, and Shayne's little heap of souvenirs. He must be in his middle fifties, Shayne thought, but he looked younger. He was lean and hard, with a heavily ruled face and piercing black eyes.

"Give him a drink if he wants one, Stevens," he said to the big man. "I'll let you know when I need you."

All they had was whiskey. It wasn't good whiskey. Shayne asked for soda, but they didn't have soda. He didn't bother to ask for ice, knowing they wouldn't have that either. After handing Shayne the warm drink, Stevens went into a bedroom, closing the door. There was one other bedroom; that door was also closed. A jazz record revolved on an open phonograph, the sound turned down to a faint mutter. The TV picture was on, with no sound coming from the set. On the small flickering screen, a tongue-tied Western badman was silently holding up a stagecoach.

Shayne sampled the drink. He had drunk worse whiskey, but not lately.

Manners spilled the money out of Curt's wallet. "You could have helped yourself, Shayne. There's a couple of thousand here. Wasn't it enough for you?"

"That's not how I make my living," Shayne said.

"All right, what's the proposition?"

Shayne put the watered whiskey on the floor so he wouldn't forget what he was doing and drink any more. He was on a battered sofa facing the TV set. The bandit, completing the holdup, swung onto his horse and galloped quietly away.

"First," Shayne said, "I want you to tell me how you knew where I was going to be so you could pick me up, or try to. Second, I want you to give me Maggie Smith."

Manners' eyes, fixed on Shayne's face, didn't shift. "Sam

Toby told me it would be a good idea to get you out of town. I don't know why. He said we could catch you as you left Senator Hitchcock's. That's your first point. Now who is Maggie Smith?"

"You don't know?"

"That's correct. I don't know."

"She runs a theatre here, and works for Toby on the side. You know how people like Toby are when they're being investigated. They feel a lot more comfortable if they can get a picture of the chairman of the committee in bed with somebody he's not married to. Maggie had that just about organized when I showed up. I've got a temporary postponement, but Hitchcock refuses to listen to anything I tell him about the woman. I want it canceled from your end."

Manners' face had tightened. "I have nothing to do with any of that."

"Maybe not. But you're paying the bills, and if anything goes wrong, it's your neck."

After hesitating briefly, Manners said, "All right, you can consider it canceled."

"Call him while I'm here," Shayne said. "And just so you won't call him again the minute I leave, I want a letter of apology from you to Hitchcock. To the effect that you knew nothing about this thing Toby has been setting up, and you're deeply shocked. You'd rather give up your contract than be a party to anything so slimy. I won't deliver it unless I have to."

"Toby won't like that," Manners said through thin lips.

"He won't like what he reads in the papers tomorrow morning any better."

The detective took out the keys to the big Buick and tossed them to Manners, who caught them neatly with one hand. "The three of them are tied up in the back seat. If you don't want to know where the car is parked, I'll be glad to tell the cops."

"Maybe I'll let you keep them. They didn't do such a bang-up job on you."

Shayne explained patiently, "Morrie has a broken arm, an empty shoulder holster and no license to carry a gun in

71

the District of Columbia. It wouldn't surprise me if his fingerprints are on file. Rebman and the car can both be traced to you. I didn't have any rope or adhesive tape, so I used Cheryl's stockings and tore up her skirt. You probably know how much else she was wearing—it wasn't much. The papers are going to eat this up. It's mysterious, and there's sex in it."

Shayne and Manners had been equally unsmiling so far, but suddenly, at the thought of how the livelier newspapers would cover this story, the redhead gave a hoot of laughter.

"Very funny," Manners commented.

He thought for a minute, then pulled the phone toward him and dialed a number. On the TV screen, an announcer was holding up a pack of cigarettes, moving his lips in praise of his sponsor's product. The redhead broke out his own cigarettes and offered one to Manners.

"I don't smoke," Manners said brusquely, and snapped into the phone, "Toby? I don't want to talk on your line. Call me back as soon as you can get to another phone."

He hung up. "Rebman had instructions to hire you if necessary. He decided you were too drunk to be approached on that basis. He was ready to go as high as fifteen. I'll raise it to twenty."

"Twenty thousand or twenty million?"

Manners looked pained. "Needless to say, not twenty million."

"To do what?"

"First are you interested?"

"I'm always interested in that kind of dough."

The phone rang. "Yes," Manners said. "All right, Sam. Your idea about Mike Shayne backfired, and backfired badly. Never mind how it happened. We have to pick up the pieces. He's in a position to make one or two demands. Have you been using somebody named Maggie Smith on Hitchcock?"

He listened, breaking in sharply after a moment. "Don't tell me about it. I want it scratched. Do it as soon as I hang up. If she doesn't answer her phone, ring her doorbell, and

72

keep at it till you wake her up. Tell her to stay away from Hitchcock, starting now. That's all. Keep in touch."

Shayne motioned to him.

"Hold it," Manners said into the phone. "What is it, Shayne?"

"Ask him how much he agreed to pay her."

Manners repeated the question to Toby and hung up after listening to the answer.

"He's promoting a foundation grant for her theatre," he said. "It could run as high as thirty thousand."

Shayne felt an unreasoning stab of disappointment. Even now, he realized, he had been hoping it would turn out that Maggie had been telling the truth and everybody else had been lying.

Manners took a lined memo pad out of one of the manila folders. "I don't like Sam Toby," he said, biting off the words, "and this is the last time I deal with him. What do you want me to say to Hitchcock?"

"Put it in your own words," Shayne said. "Mike Shayne tells you that a woman named Maggie Smith has been working on him, and Toby confirms it. Toby's arranging some financing for her theatre in return. This isn't the way you like to work. You gave Toby hell and told him to call it off, and you're glad you caught it this early, before any harm was done."

Manners scrawled a message covering half a page. He tore it off and tossed it to Shayne. Shayne read it, nodded and put it away. He kept his face impassive, but all the alarm bells were clanging. They shouldn't have been so ready to jettison Maggie Smith. Something was wrong here, and he didn't know what. On the record player another jazz record came down and began to spin. There was an unmistakable note of menace in the air.

"We thought you were working for National," Manners said. "But you've actually been working for Hitchcock's family, haven't you? I understand he has a daughter?"

Shayne shrugged and started to get up. Manners went on, "To be candid, I wouldn't want to hire you away from a competitor, because I couldn't be sure you wouldn't try to get away with drawing a fee from both sides. But I assume that this wraps it up as far as you're concerned. We need some background on Senator Tom Wall. We suspect he's on the National payroll. He's close to Henry Clark, who handles National's undercover lobbying. We need proof of this, and we need it in a hurry. The payment schedule would be —two thousand down, eighteen thousand balance on delivery of something we can use."

Shayne picked up his drink, looked at it with distaste and set it back on the floor.

"That sounds possible. But you'd better get somebody who can find the Washington Monument without having to follow a cab driver. Probably there's no reason you shouldn't know—Trina Hitchcock hired me to keep her father out of bed with the Smith woman. And that's all she hired me to do. I've been working on something in Miami the last few days and I'm behind on my sleep. Now I'm going to start catching up. As soon as the hearings adjourn I'm going back to a town where the cops know me and I have friends on the papers. That makes a difference."

Manners screwed on the top of his fountain pen and clipped it to his shirt pocket. "Has it occurred to you that you might have been brought to Washington for some other reason than the one you were given?"

"Let's say it's occurred to me." Shayne crossed the uncarpeted floor and added his cigarette butt to the others in the ashtray. "But the hell with it. The day's over."

"I'd like to take another minute to give you some history," Manners said. "Sit down and finish your drink."

Shayne returned to the sofa. "OK, but I'm having trouble keeping my eyes open."

"One year ago I had my back to the wall. I'd made the mistake of putting too much time into building airplanes and too little into buttering up the generals and admirals. The fat cats at National thought the time was ripe to take me over. Two of their top executives and three of their directors are ex-general officers, and their only company duty is to stay on friendly terms with their ex-colleagues in the Pentagon. I've never gone in for that old-buddy crap. I'd never heard the name of Sam Toby. If he'd come into my office and said I needed to hire a Washington influence peddler to stay in business, I would have thrown him out on his ear. Then National took a contract away from me after I'd spent two million on wind-tunnel tests. I had a couple of big loans called, for no good reason. All of a sudden my credit sources dried up. I began to hear that rumors were going around about me personally—my financial position, even my sanity. National made me an offer. The price was ridiculous. I turned it down. They began raiding my stock, and drove it down to below nine dollars a share. All the analysts were predicting I'd be in bankruptcy in six months. They hadn't seen my books. I had six weeks."

"And what does all this have to do with me?" Shayne said blurrily.

"Manners common closed this afternoon at one hundred and ten. I have thirty thousand men at work in five states. We've had enough delays. We're finally rolling on this plane, and anything that holds us up now will be bad for everybody. There's no question of canceling the contract. It's too late for that. The reason National is making this big effort is to show they still have some political muscle, to lay the groundwork for the next time. No matter how big you are, you have to wade through a certain amount of mud to get a contract like this one. The reason I'm fighting Hitchcock's investigation is that I don't want any of the mud splattered on the airplane. Who made what promises, who paid what legal fees, who traded what favors for what phone calls— none of that matters, Shayne. What matters is how far can the plane fly without refueling? How fast? How much load can it carry? How soon will it be operational?"

"Well, as I say—" Shayne said.

Manners put his hands flat on the table and pushed himself erect, and Shayne realized that the industrialist must need sleep almost as much as he did himself.

"You've done what you were brought in to do," Manners said evenly. "Pleasant dreams. Here." He held out the whiskey bottle, which was still three-quarters full. "Take this with you. The bars close at two and you'll have trouble getting a drink. What I'm trying to get across is this: Rebman did badly tonight. But he's a capable man, and don't underestimate him. Think about my offer. It'll still be open in the morning. If anybody else tops it, bear in mind that there's nothing I won't do, and I mean that literally, to put that airplane into production. Don't get in the way."

"Hell," Shayne said, "I'm getting out of it as fast as I can. I don't go around looking for trouble."

"Where do we find the Buick?"

"Around the corner from a spot called the Bijou on Wisconsin. I don't know the name of the street."

"Stevens!" Manners called.

The big man came out of the bedroom and Manners said, "Shayne's leaving."

Manners and the redhead exchanged a look. They obviously respected each other, but they made no move to shake hands. One of the things Shayne was wondering was who had smoked the cigarettes in Manners' ashtray. He grinned at Stevens and said, "Mind if I use your bathroom?"

He took two long strides and opened the other bedroom door. He heard someone moving and smelled cigarette smoke, but all he could see was a raincoat and a brown felt hat on one of a pair of twin beds. Then Stevens, moving fast, took the doorknob out of his hand.

"Mr. Manners has things to do."

"I won't insist," Shayne said peaceably.

Manners was watching him. The phone had begun to ring, but he made no move to answer it until the redhead half waved and went out. Manners was clearly not finished for the night, and neither was Shayne. He had been watching the polished performance of an accomplished magician; his eye had been misdirected, so he had been looking the wrong way when the substitution was made. If he went to bed now, he would wake up in the morning to find that something surprising and possibly ugly had happened.

"Terrific, isn't he?" Stevens said on the stairs.

"Yeah," Shayne agreed. "I don't know if I'd like to have

him around all the time. It would be like living with a band-saw."

"Oh, he's OK if you do what he says. When you're working for Manners you don't sit around wondering who's boss. He's got that big company in the palm of his hand, like this." He clenched his fist, which was the size of a small cantaloupe. "Rebman, now, Mr. Manners is going to take off his hide in strips."

They said goodnight, and Stevens stayed in the doorway until Shayne got into his Ford and drove away. Manners had obviously been conferring with someone when Shayne arrived, driving the visitor into the bedroom. It was a clear, hot night, with no sign of rain, so why, Shayne wondered, had the visitor been wearing a raincoat?

He circled the block. Turning back onto 16th, he parked across from the Royalton Arms. There was a similar apartment house on the opposite corner, with an equally flossy name, the Pickwick. He went into the lighted lobby, unscrewed the overhead bulb so he couldn't be seen from the street, and waited.

Presently Stevens came out, squeezed into a compact sedan and drove off, probably to rescue Cheryl and the others from the locked Buick. Shayne dozed, leaning against the mailboxes, snapping awake abruptly as the door across the street opened again. This time it was a short, burly figure wearing the raincoat and felt hat Shayne had seen in Manners' bedroom. The raincoat collar was turned up, the hat brim was turned down. Not much showed in between except the burning spark of a cigarette.

When he went around the building, Shayne left the lobby and slid into his Ford. A moment later he heard the roar of a powerful unmuffled motor. A squat black English sedan came out of the driveway. The man had taken off his disguise getting into his car. The raincoat had concealed an Air Force uniform. Light glinted from the insignia on his shoulders; they were eagles.

Shayne waited a moment so the colonel wouldn't know he was being followed. That was Shayne's only hope, for the

English car had a fast acceleration and considerable power. Shayne managed to hang on for several miles, while they made their way north and west, toward Virginia. He could not work close enough to be sure of the license number.

On Connecticut Avenue, Shayne was held up for a moment by a turning truck. It was a big tractor and trailer, and there was nothing Shayne could do but wait. While it was inching out of his way, the colonel turned off to the right into a maze of side streets. There Shayne lost him.

THE PHONE RANG A LONG TIME. IT WAS ANSWERED BY TWO voices, a fraction of a second apart. One was the Swedish maid, the other Trina Hitchcock.

"Miss Hitchcock?" Shayne said. "Michael Shayne. Will you get the maid off the extension?"

"Michael?" she said vaguely. "Michael Shayne. I have it, Hanna, this is my call."

There was a click as the maid hung up. Trina said, "You'll have to start over. I took a pill and I'm not quite in focus. You aren't still working?"

"Yeah, I'm still working. The Maggie Smith thing seems to be taken care of. But I don't like the way it happened—it was too easy."

"Too easy? Mr. Shayne, you aren't getting through to me. Is she leaving town?"

"It doesn't matter if she does or not. I've got a written admission from Hugh Manners of what she was doing for them and how they were paying her. It won't hang anybody, but your father can't pretend he doesn't understand it. I don't want to show it to him yet. I'd like to let him go on thinking she went out with him because she liked him. Maybe I'll send her a copy and tell her I'll use it if she tries to get in touch with him again. She's been yanked off by Toby, more or less in my hearing, and I think that probably winds it up."

"Mr. Shayne!" Trina wailed. "Have pity! You're going too fast. How in heaven's name did you get an admission out of Hugh Manners? I can hardly believe it. But there's no need for you to hang around indefinitely. Why don't we consider that your part is finished? Give me the letter or whatever it is. I'll keep my eyes open. If Daddy shows any signs of doing anything foolish, I'll let him see it."

"It's not that simple," Shayne said. "Manners sent three people after me, two men and a girl. The girl was wearing a two-hundred-dollar dress. They offered me a large hunk of money and took a swipe at me with a blackjack. And right after that they gave me Maggie Smith without batting an eye. There's something phony about it."

"A blackjack, a two-hundred-dollar dress—my head's spinning. What does it mean?"

"I wish I knew, Miss Hitchcock. I think they have something else underway, which probably involves your father. I also think they don't want me around when it happens. Do you know how I can get in touch with Senator Wall?"

"He lives at the Park Plaza, but he won't thank you for waking him up at two in the morning."

"I'll take a chance. Thanks."

"Mr. Shayne—" she said quickly.

He waited. After a moment she said, "Well, frankly I don't understand it. It's cold comfort to be told that you don't either. I'm in no position to give you orders, though, so goodnight."

"Goodnight."

He looked up the Park Plaza and dialed the number. The switchboard girl connected him with the night manager, who explained that they had a policy of not ringing their guests' rooms after midnight without advance authorization, and would Mr. Shayne care to leave a message?

Shayne said, "I'm calling on Senate business, and it's important. Can you tell me whether or not he's in his room? If he hasn't come in yet I won't waste any time arguing."

"One moment." When the voice returned to the line, it reported flatly but with a faint note of surprise, "Senator Wall is out."

Shayne's exhausted body was telling him to call it quits, but he forced himself to keep going. He looked up Ronald Bixler's address; the little Civil Service investigator might know where he could start looking for Wall. Then he dialed Trina Hitchcock's number again.

She picked up the phone promptly.

"Shayne again. Sorry to keep bothering you, but Senator Wall hasn't come in."

"That's funny. He's a stickler about how much sleep he gets, and with that big hearing in the morning—"

"Probably that's what he's working on. Did he give you any idea of where he might be?"

"No, it was very cloak-and-dagger and hush-hush, that's the way Tom is. But I still don't see why you're so anxious to talk to him."

"I don't think he knows Manners is in town. I know where he can be found if Wall wants to hit him with a subpoena, but it has to be done now. I doubt if he'll still be there in the morning."

"Why should anybody want to subpoena Manners? It's Sam Toby they're investigating. I assure you, Tom Wall knows what he's doing, and in any event I'm not in his confidence."

"Will you wake up your father for me?"

"I wouldn't think of it. Mr. Shayne, in fairness, this isn't really your forte, is it? You've taken care of Maggie Smith, and you seem to have done it thoroughly and well. Daddy's on the alert now and nothing so terrible is going to happen. Now don't make any more trouble. Go home."

"What do you call trouble?" Shayne said softly.

"I didn't mean that. I know I'm not making any sense. But I engaged you to do something specific, the kind of thing experience has fitted you for. You've done it. Why isn't it over? Of course I want you to consider that whatever is left of that ten thousand dollars is your fee, and please accept it without arguing."

"Is it your money, Miss Hitchcock?"

"What are you implying by that? Of course it's my money. Mr. Shayne—isn't it barely possible that some of these interrelationships may be more than you can hope to work out in a couple of hours?"

"Barely possible," Shayne said wryly.

"And that by bulling around blindfolded, the way you've been doing, you may be doing more harm than good? Right now my father may not appreciate what you've done. Probably he let fly some fairly caustic observations about meddling busybodies, et cetera, but someday when he can think back on this period in tranquility, he'll give you credit for preserving him from the stupidest blunder an old man can make. Now will you go home?"

"I'll think about it," Shayne said.

"Do. Now I intend to take another pill. Goodnight again."

Shayne had promised to think about it, and he thought about it for fully a minute after he hung up. Then, swearing savagely under his breath, he put himself back together and left the booth.

CHAPTER 10
2:10 A.M.

RONALD BIXLER LIVED IN A LARGE ANONYMOUS CONCRETE-and-glass apartment house in the Southwest redevelopment area. Shayne hesitated after finding his name and apartment number in the lobby. At this hour an urgent knock on the door would stand a better chance of being answered than the ringing of a doorbell.

Using a strip of celluloid that he carried in his wallet, he opened the inner door. An automatic elevator took him up nine floors. He found Bixler's apartment. Music was playing softly inside and he heard voices.

He knocked sharply. The voices stopped. He was facing a small round one-way mirror, and there was a faint clatter as it opened on the inside.

The door was thrown open promptly. Bixler, his face red, his eyes bulging, was wearing a kind of smoking jacket with velvet lapels. On a mannequin in a store window it had probably looked quietly dashing. It was wrong for Bixler.

"Mike Shayne!" he cried with his slight lisp. "This is what I call a pleasant surprith! Come in, Mike, and join us in a glass of cold champagne."

His apartment was furnished simply, with good modern furniture. A big picture window looked out at the lights along the Potomac. There were two champagne glasses on a glass-topped table, a few lipstick-tipped cigarette ends in the ashtray, but no other sign of Bixler's guest.

"I hope I'm not butting in," Shayne said.

"Absolutely not. There's always a welcome for Mike Shayne in my humble—ah, pad. I've been entertaining, because what would life be like without the ladies? She's a little shy." Lowering his voice, he said confidentially, "It's the first time I ever had her up here." He knocked at the closed bathroom door. "It's OK to come out, Margaret. It's Mike Shayne. The one I was telling you about."

A faint voice inside said, "Tell me as soon as he's gone."

"I want you to meet him! I know it's late, but you don't have to worry—Mike's been around."

When there was no answer, Bixler shrugged.

"Make yourself at home, Michael. If I'd thought there was a faint chance you might be dropping by, I would have laid in a supply of Markell's. Isn't that what you drink? Or is it Martell's?"

He twirled the champagne bottle ceremoniously in its bucket and filled a glass for Shayne. "See what you think of this bubbly. The man at the store said I couldn't do better at twice the money."

He beamed after Shayne tasted the champagne and nodded approvingly.

"Do you live it up like this every night?" Shayne asked. "Working for the government must be a better deal than I thought."

Bixler laughed heartily. "That's good, Mike. No, working for the government is financially very unrewarding, if you don't count in the fringe benefits. This is a celebration."

"You've started spending the two thousand bucks I gave you?"

Bixler touched his finger to his lips, sending a meaningful glance at the bathroom door. "I'm celebrating two things. The second thing was even more satisfactory, both to ye olde bank account and my self-esteem. A small financial token of esteem from a certain senator who must here remain nameless, but whose name begins with—" He sketched the letter W in the air. "I didn't bargain. I named a price and then I was like granite. I just smiled quietly. Finally he paid it."

"I hope this wasn't the same information you sold me."

"Certainly not. I never sell anything twice. That way you can make enemies."

"I'm trying to find Wall. Do you know where he might be?"

"I think I can make an educated guess." He went back to

the bathroom door and rapped again. "Margaret, don't be like that. Come on out."

The door opened in a moment and a plain, dumpy woman emerged. She was stiff and embarrassed. Two pinch-marks on the bridge of her nose showed that she habitually wore glasses, though she had taken them off in honor of the champagne.

"Margaret, I'd like to have you meet the famous Mike Shayne," Bixler announced, "in person. Mike, this is Miss Saul, my secretary. She's in the pool, really, but I always ask for her, and do you blame me?"

"I certainly don't," Shayne said.

"How do you do," Miss Saul said, looking no higher than Shayne's necktie. "Ron, it's so late I really think I must be going."

Bixler tried to talk her into letting him fill her glass, but she insisted. She also refused to let him change his jacket and escort her home.

"I live downstairs on the sixth floor, you see, Mr. Shayne," she explained, blushing.

Stooping swiftly, she retrieved a white bracelet from the floor near the sofa. Blushing more violently, she said, "I had a perfectly lovely evening, Ron. See you at work tomorrow."

He took her to the door, where he whispered something. She giggled and gave him a push. He was preening himself when he came back.

"A very warm person, Mike. No raving beauty, I'll be the first to admit, but the truth of the matter is that I think surface prettiness is greatly overrated in women. Bosoms—people believe in these great enormous bosoms, but I for one think companionability's more important. You're used to the women in the sensual south. You wouldn't believe how puritanical they can be in this town. This apartment is setting me back an arm and a leg, but it'll be worth it if tonight's any example. More champagne?"

He filled Shayne's glass and raised his own. "Here's to money."

Shayne started to speak, but Bixler forestalled him.

"Michael, I just wanted to say this. I know you want to locate Senator Wall, so you can confer about overall strategy, and the reason you dropped by is that you've figured out that I know that—" He stopped, confused. "I seem to be a little —but don't worry, I know what I'm trying to say, I have a good head for liquor. What I mean is, I'm under no illusion that this is a social visit. You have an ulterior motive, like everybody, and you're probably impatient to get moving. I know how monotonous it must be, always running into people who are sort of like disciples, but I'm a dyed-in-the-wool disciple of yours and I always have been. You're the reason I took up investigation in the first place. Maybe it didn't work out the way I expected, but that's no fault of yours. That's Washington. It's been tedious, and the financial pickings have been slim. Not many glamorous women have come my way. And then you blew in, and in six hours I made more money than in the whole last year. Margaret sensed the change right away. That made the difference between coming up for a drink and not coming up for a drink. Where was I?"

"Weren't you about to tell me what it was you sold Wall?"

"I guess I was. He told me not to breathe a word to a soul, but that wouldn't include *you*. If you want to check further, and knowing your methods I think you will, you may be able to find him at Oskar's, that's an after-hours joint, 17 Larue Place, off Ninth Street, pretty sleazy. That's the first place I'd try if I was you."

"I'm surprised he's still making the rounds," Shayne said. "I heard he usually gets to bed early when he's going to be working the next day."

"Oh, this is no pub-crawling expedition," Bixler told him. "Wall? Heavens, no. He wouldn't be caught dead in that kind of joint if he didn't think there was money in it. You know that as well as I do."

"I don't know anything at all about these people," Shayne said. "That's why I came to see you."

Bixler broke into a happy smile. "Think of being in a position to give pointers to Mike Shayne! You're going to be calling me Ron before the evening's over, aren't you, Mike?"

"It wouldn't surprise me," Shayne said agreeably. "What does this all go back to, something you found out when you were investigating Toby for the Hitchcock committee?"

"There! You don't beat around the bush, like some people. You put your finger right on the crucial point. I'll tell it in chronological order, that would be the best way."

He took a large gulp of champagne. "This was just before I went with Civil Service—well, I told you that. I was working for Hitchcock, if you can call it working. We had half a dozen things we were supposed to be looking into, and Toby was one of them. He's a perennial. We weren't any of us too eager. Step on the wrong toes in something like that and before you know it you'll be lining up for unemployment insurance. So before you even call up and make an appointment to see somebody, better check to make sure you got the right kind of backing."

"That must make it hard to operate," Shayne put in.

"It does. But you have to remember that nobody in Congress likes these investigations, never mind on which side of the aisle. Because they can run away. We all knew nobody really wanted Sam Toby at that point. We weren't feeling any pressure from the papers or anybody. They keep that subcommittee 'way understaffed, and if I'd really been working on all the things I was supposed to be working on, I'd need six assistants and twenty-five pairs of hands. Well, there was this certain prominent woman named Mrs. Masterson, who had a Georgetown house and did a lot of entertaining. Those parties were the chic thing for a while. I didn't see her allure, myself. We were speaking about female bosoms here a minute ago, and hers, to be frank with you, was a little excessive. One of the ten best-dressed Washington women. Maybe not too puritanical in her private life, if there was sufficient scratch on the line. Well, we got this tip that she was getting some financial backing from Mr. Toby, I won't go into all the ins and outs. Usually, as I said, I wouldn't follow up that sort of lead unless I was told to in writing, but this one was giving off a strong money-odor, and on my own initiative, and being very careful, believe me, I was looking into it. I'm being candid with you, Mike, you would have done the same thing in my shoes. I thought if I could tie her to Toby it would be worth something not to pass it on to the committee. I mean, the country wasn't exactly clamoring for an exposé, plus the fact that the situation wouldn't be changed one iota even if we succeeded in putting him in jail."

"Nobody else knew you were working on it?"

"I had to cover myself, you understand. Working's the wrong word—every so often I'd make a phone call, if I was in a certain neighborhood I'd drop in on somebody. Now it happened that Mrs. Masterson had a fight with her maid and fired her, and I heard about it. I looked up the maid and gave her a song and dance about how it was her patriotic duty to tell me everything she knew about the lady. I was disappointed to hear that she hadn't slept in. What happened after dark was what I mainly wanted to know. The girl was a Polack, Olga Szep, with a *z*. Not bad looking, a bit on the husky side. The name's fresh in my mind because her brother runs the place I was telling you about, Oskar's. She works there waiting on table."

"I don't want you to think I'm not following you, Ron, but let's finish up with what happened last year."

"How's your champagne holding out? There may be a dividend at the bottom."

"You take it," Shayne said.

"Well, if yours is OK, I believe I will. When I get a buzz going I hate to let it fade out on me." He shook the last drops of champagne into his glass. "To make a long story short, Mrs. Masterson kept a diary! To protect herself, I suppose, because Toby has a reputation for using somebody just so long, and then when the wrinkles begin to show— kaput, finish."

"You're sure it was a diary?"

"That's what it said on the outside, according to Olga, 'My Diary,' and she kept it locked in her jewel box. At that moment in history I hadn't had a raise for eighteen months. Side money—you know, odds and ends—was all that kept me going. Mike, maybe right now I'd better get your promise. This has to be strictly between you and me."

Shayne's eyes were bleak. "I never make that kind of promise."

"You don't?" Bixler said, dashed. "Couldn't you stretch a point in my case?"

"I'm sorry, Ron. I make that a rule."

"Not that I committed any crime. I'm just trying to establish motivation. I didn't clear one cent out of this until tonight, and that's perfectly ethical. But at the time, in a situation that was pregnant with possibilities, I admit I began thinking of how I could turn it into cash. Did Olga know where Mrs. Masterson kept her keys? She did. Was she sore enough about being fired, or to put it another way, the way I actually put it to Olga, was she devoted enough to the internal security of the United States, to borrow that diary for half an hour so I could see if there were any government secrets in it? And she was! All she wanted was fifteen hundred dollars, believe it or not. Probably no more than a gradeschool education, no imagination at all. Of course she didn't know about Mrs. Masterson's Toby connection, and how much he grosses in fees and commissions. If things broke right, if I could sell that diary to Toby, I could retire from the government and open my own office, which has always been my ambition."

"And if they didn't break right, you might end up in the morgue."

"Hardly. Toby's done just about everything else, but he's never killed anybody as far as I know." He finished his glass. "You know champagne could get to be a pretty expensive habit?"

"And then what happened?" Shayne prompted.

"Then my Civil Service appointment came through. Finally, after hanging fire for months and months. Ronald Bixler, report to the Chicago office without delay. Well, I griped and I groused all the way to Chicago, but maybe subconsciously I was relieved. Going up against Toby with this material—I know my limitations. He would have smiled me out of it, or twisted it around some way. But I couldn't just drop it after I'd developed it that far, could I? I said to myself I'd come back the next weekend and finish it up. And when I came back the next weekend, Olga Szep had made herself scarce. She'd dropped out of the scene altogether. I tried to find her for two days, but she didn't want to be found."

"How did you interpret that?"

"Either she'd caught a slight case of cold feet, or she'd decided she didn't need me, and tried for more than the fifteen hundred. Well, an amateur like Olga against Sam Toby's organization? That would be the mismatch of the century. I decided the better part of valor was not to ask too many questions. I did ask one of the guys on the committee staff what happened to the Toby investigation, and they'd all been pulled off. It could be that the fix was in, or maybe it was legitimate, who knows? I never decided how much hanky-panky there was in that, if any."

"How long did you stay in Chicago?"

"Till last month. This I wangled, because in the back of my mind I've never forgotten Mrs. Masterson's diary. Would you, in my shoes? So when Senator Wall looked me up—*he* looked *me* up—I knew right away what he was talking about and how to proceed."

"Did he have anything to do with the investigation last year?"

"He had access to the files. More than that I don't know. We felt each other out. I was still a little leery, but as soon as he told me there were National Aviation funds available, it solved my problem."

"I don't think I get that, Ron."

"I mean I could sell it in that quarter without risk. Dealing with Toby, eyeball to eyeball—well, I don't know if I have the stature for it, frankly. It just so happened that I knew where they could contact Olga and take it from there, because the minute I got transferred back from Chicago I went to work on it. I ran down about ninety blind leads until I came across the right one. It turned out that she'd been away. One of her brothers—she has two, both apes—owned this joint, and when she came back to town she went to work for him. I dropped in one night to look it over. She let out a yell, recognized me right away. Her brothers walked me to the door and gave me a kick in the slats to remember them by. I'm not like you, Mike. I don't keep fit. I had to let them get away with it."

"You didn't find out why she went out of town, or where?"

"Mike, they didn't let me utter more than two or three words. OK, what should I do now? I decided that doing nothing might be the best bet. But it kept gnawing at me. It took away my peace of mind. And then in walked Senator Wall, out of the blue, so to speak. I brought him up to date and sold him Olga's address. I made it clear—no public testifying, because I value my rating. Gee," he said abruptly, "maybe I made a mistake taking that last drink. I have a tremendous capacity for liquor, but isn't there something about the dregs at the bottom of a wine bottle?"

"Ron, stay with me another minute. Did this Mrs. Masterson ever have anything to do with an Air Force colonel?"

Bixler fell against the arm of the sofa. "Snuck up on me. Millions of Air Force colonels."

"This one's about five-ten, broad through the shoulders—"

Bixler waved his hand to stir up the air in front of him. "Funny thing. All I can see is bubbles."

"Is Mrs. Masterson still in Washington?"

He fixed Shayne with an eye that suddenly seemed off-center. "Not in the papers any more. Going to find out first thing in the morning. Child's play for experienced investigator. Maybe there's more money in this. Could be, you know."

He stood up, his hand to his mouth. " 'Scuse me, Michael. With you in a minute."

He headed for the bathroom in an S-shaped line, taking the last few feet at a run. He slammed the door. Shayne waited, listening to the bathroom noises, then made up his mind and let himself out.

CHAPTER 11
2:45 A.M.

ACCUMULATED FATIGUE CAUGHT UP WITH MICHAEL SHAYNE as he got into his car. Heavy weights pulled at his eyelids. His hands suddenly became too heavy to lift. For an instant, as he sat at the wheel, willing himself to turn the key, he went to sleep. Wall, Hitchcock, Sam Toby, Trina, Maggie Smith—they were like scattered pieces of a jigsaw puzzle, and as he slept they shifted about and changed places, turning over and over. He seized each in turn and made it hold still. Even then nothing would fit.

He snapped awake. The car seemed to start itself and glide away from the curb with no help from Shayne. He was finally beginning to adjust to Washington's pattern of avenues and circles. A short drive north brought him to the Capitol, and after that it was no problem to find Connecticut Avenue and the Park Plaza Hotel. Leaving the Ford double-parked, he asked at the desk if Senator Wall was in. Again the answer was no.

He lit a cigarette after getting back in his car. At some point, he knew, Bixler had stopped telling the truth and started lying. He had sold one set of facts to Shayne, another to Senator Wall. In spite of his denials, had he sold still a third to Toby?

The detective smoked the cigarette down to the stub before deciding that, late as it was, he had to tell Hitchcock what he had learned. Bixler had worked for Hitchcock's committee. If he had been dealing with Toby, Hitchcock should know about it. Not in the morning, but right now.

Sighing, Shayne tried to get his bearings. He turned the wrong way on Massachusetts Avenue, realizing his mistake after several blocks. He was relieved to see the big mounted statue of General Sheridan. He knew his way from there.

He was surprised to see the lights still on in Hitchcock's house. As he slowed, he heard a car door slam. Fully awake now, he accelerated, cut in sharply, then slammed on his brakes. The car that was backing out of the Hitchcock driveway, a big station wagon, slithered to a stop inches away from his front fender.

A woman wearing dark glasses, with a scarf tied over her hair, craned out the window. "Move your car, please," she said, in a voice that showed she was used to having her suggestions followed. "You're blocking me."

Shayne got out to look the situation over. "Yeah, you're right."

She raced her motor angrily. "Do you want me to ram into you?"

"That might work," Shayne admitted. "Your car's heavier than mine."

"Is this some kind of joke?" she demanded. "Move out of my way this instant or I'll call the police."

"You wouldn't really do that," the redhead said politely. "Would you mind taking off your dark glasses? I just want to be sure you're Mrs. Redpath before I say the wrong thing."

She took out her feelings on the motor, racing it violently. "Damn it, you only saw me for ten minutes. It's dark, and I hoped you wouldn't recognize me. Please, Mr. Shayne, I can't talk to you now."

Shayne grinned at her. "You were friendlier the last time I saw you. You even said you'd help if there was anything I didn't understand. Mrs. Redpath, there's hardly anything I *do* understand."

"I said that hours and hours and hours ago." Her voice climbed. *"Will you get out of my way?"*

Shayne went on grinning. "I've been wondering what your husband did for Sam Toby on that Manners contract, and why. That's what you've been talking to Hitchcock about, isn't it?"

She managed to control herself, but the effort showed. She took off her dark glasses.

"I understand you've been doing all right without any

help." Drawing a quick breath, she produced a fairly presentable smile, though her arms and shoulders were still tense. "My husband doesn't know I'm here. I hate to think what would happen if he wakes up before I get back. Senator Hitchcock can explain. If there's anything else you need to know, come to see me in the morning. I'll arrange to be alone."

She smiled again, and this time it looked more real. With her foot on the brake, her skirt had slipped back from her knee. Her legs were brown and slender. She was effective, and she knew it.

Shayne said stubbornly, "This will only take a minute. I need the answers right now."

Her smile departed. "You won't get them! I can't answer that kind of question on the spur of the moment! I need some advice first."

"Legal advice?"

She switched off the motor and hauled at the emergency brake. "I can't make you move. At the same time I don't think you're sure enough of yourself to hold me by force. I'll find a taxi."

She unlatched the door. Shayne shut it again.

"I'll give you some advice, Mrs. Redpath. If you can't help being anxious, don't let it show so much."

"You know nothing whatever about it!" she snapped.

"God knows that's true."

He returned to his Ford and backed out of her way. She came past him, stopping when the two cars were parallel.

"Shall I expect you in the morning?" she said in a low voice.

"Maybe. It depends on what I find out in the meantime."

"Leave one or two things for me to clear up. I'm sorry I screamed at you—I should have known better. Goodnight."

After she was gone, Shayne backed in against the curb and parked. His face was thoughtful. He opened the door and got out. Stevens, the big man who took care of letting people in and out of Hugh Manners' apartment, was waiting for him.

He looked relaxed and deadly, like a sleeping rattle-snake. "Mr. Manners thought you'd be turning up here, Shayne. He wants to talk some more. He doesn't think you leveled with him the last time."

Without turning, Shayne knew that somebody else had materialized behind him. His only chance was to move fast.

"Always glad to talk to Mr. Manners," he said easily, and swung from the heels.

He put his full weight into the punch. It exploded at the point of Stevens' jaw. The big man's relaxed smile slackened. Shayne grasped the front of his shirt and pulled, pivoting. Now he saw the other man, a Mexican, wearing a loose, brightly patterned sports shirt. He had his hand inside his belt, but he wasn't quick enough. The big man plowed into him, his arms windmilling. He was already on his way down, and he took the Mexican with him. Shayne stepped in close and kicked the gun out of the Mexican's hand. Another kick sent it under the nearest car.

Stevens was still partially conscious. The other man pawed at him, trying to push him off. Shayne knew he didn't have time to cramp his car out of its tight berth; there was too good a chance that Stevens also had a gun, and his head would clear soon enough to use it. Shayne plunged into Hitchcock's driveway and across the garden, making for the back wall. From a lighted window at the rear of the house Trina Hitchcock called peremptorily, "Is that you, Shayne? Mike Shayne!"

Shayne hit the brick wall without breaking stride, straightening to his full height as his body hurtled upward. He caught the top of the wall with both hands. In one fluid motion he was up and over.

He dropped into somebody's flower garden. He was in darkness. He felt his way along the wall to a brick barbecue pit and stepped up on it, raising his head cautiously. He was concealed from the street by the Hitchcock garage. He heard running footsteps. Swinging onto the wall, he rolled over, landing lightly. The side door to the street, which he and Hitchcock had entered by earlier, had a spring lock and could be opened from the inside.

He looked out carefully. The street was empty. By this time, if Shayne had figured correctly, Stevens and his friend were a block away, waiting to cut him off when he emerged on the next street. He checked again at the corner, feeling like a foot soldier in an enemy city. He went around fast, leaped into the Ford and hit the starter and the gas. He backed violently into the car parked behind him, then came forward, the wheel all the way over. Fenders scraped, but he broke through and roared away, the gas pedal on the floor.

He swung onto Thirty-first, shifted, and was doing seventy before he reached M Street. He turned north, tires screaming. He didn't think there was anybody behind him, but he didn't ease up until he had circled through the cloverleaf and was on the freeway, heading south along the river.

CHAPTER 12
3:10 A.M.

HE HIRED A TAXI TO LEAD HIM TO OSKAR'S, THE AFTER-HOURS club on Larue Place. After they found it, Shayne signaled the driver to follow him until he found a better place to park. Then he transferred to the cab for the brief trip back.

"Will I have any trouble getting in?"

"Not if you're not a cop," the driver said cheerfully. He was short and fat, with a dead cigar clamped between his teeth. "And a cop wouldn't have to pay cab fare to find it, would he?"

"I got the address from a bellhop," Shayne said. "It sounded OK, but I don't like the looks of the neighborhood. I never appreciate getting rolled."

"Who does? You won't get rolled inside; they run a pretty clean operation. It's after you leave you want to keep your eyes open. I mean, don't let anybody inveigle you into a hallway."

Shayne checked the license posted on the back of the front seat. The driver's name was Edward Siemanski.

"I'll buy you a drink, Ed," he suggested. "Plus a buck for your waiting time. Then we can pick up the Ford and you can show me how to get back to my hotel."

"Sure, glad to. I'm knocking off in fifteen minutes anyway."

He put up his windows and checked the locks all around after he parked. Shayne waited on the sidewalk, rattling the change in his pockets. The only indication that drinks were on sale in No. 17 was the number over the door: it was much larger and more conspicuous than the numbers on nearby buildings. The door was several steps below street level. On one side was a store selling trusses, crutches, and artificial limbs. The building on the other side was empty, with white crosses on the windows, marking it for the wreckers. On the corner there was a theatre specializing in nudist movies. Except for a prowling cat, nothing moved anywhere on the block.

"Let's go," the driver said. "And remind me to come out to look every couple of minutes, so they don't steal the paint job off me. Not that it's my cab."

He knocked at the door beneath the big 17, and a moment later it opened. This was Shayne's night for running into big men. The blond man in the doorway wasn't as tall as Stevens, but he was equally broad through the chest. He looked like a guard or a tackle on a good pro football team. A pair of muscular arms bulged out below the rolled-up sleeves of a blue work shirt. One of the forearms was tattooed with a snake and an American flag.

"Hey, Pete," the driver said. "We're thirsty."

"Eddie," the doorman replied. "Who's your friend?"

"He's OK. I only met him ten minutes ago, but from what I know about human nature, he's no cop."

The big blond gave Shayne a hard look. "That'll be one dollar membership."

Shayne paid him and they were allowed to enter a large air-conditioned room. The air was damp and clammy. Shayne glanced around quickly, without seeing Senator Wall. Several couples were dancing to music from a jukebox at the far end of the room. The customers were all surprisingly well dressed, having started the evening in other parts of town. Some of them were having a very good time, others seemed to be contemplating suicide. At this time of night there was nothing in between.

Eddie started for the bar, but Shayne pointed toward an empty table. "Let's get comfortable."

"Why not?" Eddie agreed.

A waitress came over to take their orders. Her straw-colored hair was nicely arranged and her black uniform did everything that could be done for her sturdy figure. Her arms were nearly as muscular as the doorman's. Her face also resembled his, with heavy blonde brows and craggy cheekbones.

"Old Granddad on the rocks," Eddie said.

She looked at Shayne. He said, "Isn't your name Olga Szep?"

Her reaction seemed considerably overdone. She drew in a sharp breath and put her hand to her throat.

"Now, *listen*," Eddie said. "If you've been conning me, I mean if you're working some kind of an angle here, you'd better change your mind right now. These guys are selling liquor against the law. They can't afford to kid."

"I didn't insult anybody," Shayne said. "All I did was ask her if her name was Olga Szep."

The girl's Adam's apple went up and down. Eddie called after her as she turned, "Anyway, get my bourbon."

The bartender met her at the service end of the bar. She spoke to him quietly.

"I'm going to be marked lousy in here from now on," Eddie complained. "I should have asked for your fingerprints. What did you have to pick on me for?"

"Relax," Shayne told him. "You'll get your drink. If they won't serve you, I've got a bottle of rotgut in the car."

The bartender came out, drying his hands on his apron. There was no doubt that this was a family business. He was six or seven years older than Pete, just as blond and powerful, but without the tattoos.

"Don't look at *me*, Oskar," Eddie said. "I don't know the guy from Adam. He said he got the address from a bellhop. It sounded legit."

"That was just to get in," Shayne said easily. "My name's Michael Shayne, and if you want to sell drinks the full twenty-four hours it's OK with me. I'm trying to locate a guy. From the way your sister is acting, I think he was in here earlier."

Oskar jerked his thumb toward the door. "Outside."

"In a minute," Shayne said lazily. "You probably have to pay the precinct a good percentage of the gross to stay open this late. But is that kind of street-level protection going to help you if a United States Senator has any trouble in here?"

Reaching out, he squeezed Oskar's knuckles, which were

scuffed and inflamed. Oskar jerked his hand away, wincing.

"Better put some iodine on that," Shayne said. "It's recent, isn't it?"

"What are you talking about, a United States Senator?"

"Tom Wall is his name," Shayne said, "and it's true he doesn't look like a Senator. Very wound up and jerky. Little mustache."

"No Senator come in here," Olga said sullenly.

Pete had moved into position beside his brother. The resemblance between them was very marked.

"Let's heave this guy," Oskar said. "He don't want to use his own legs, he wants to make it tough for himself."

"Before you throw me out," Shayne said, "I'd like to ask your sister a few questions about a diary."

Olga gasped. "Oskar, maybe we ought to—" she began, but her brother cut her off.

"No questions," he said savagely. "This is my place, and I make the rules." To Shayne: "Get out. On your own steam or Peter and me help you."

Shayne reached inside his coat. Pete twitched toward him. Moving slowly, the redhead took out his wallet.

"I want to pay for Eddie's drink."

He put a dollar on the table. Oskar said, "That'll be two and a quarter."

"Pour him a dollar's worth," Shayne said, standing up.

Olga, nervously plucking at her white collar, refused to meet his eyes. The jukebox was still playing, but no one was dancing.

"I'll tell you what I think happened," Shayne said. "I think Wall barged in here with his mustache going up and down and tried to get Olga to tell him what happened with Mrs. Masterson's diary. That seems to be a hot subject around here. Maybe he didn't tell you he was a Senator, or maybe you didn't believe him. You told him to shut up and go home. No Senator likes being talked to like that. They take themselves seriously. So you probably had to slug him, didn't you?"

"There wasn't any Senator," Olga repeated.

"OK, there wasn't any Senator. Give Eddie his drink."

"Why don't you go on ahead?" Eddie said. "I'll stick around and enjoy it."

Shayne shook his head curtly. He was badly outnumbered, about to be bounced, but Eddie stood up without hesitation. Oskar returned to the bar and filled a shot-glass with whiskey, which Eddie knocked back in one swallow. Pete went with them and waited till the cab was moving before going back inside.

"I told you," Eddie said. "You have to be careful with those guys."

"I was careful. Let's look around. Just cruise."

"You really think they bounced a *Senator*?"

"They bounced somebody. The blood on his knuckles isn't dry yet. That happened in the last half-hour."

Eddie drove slowly to the corner. At a signal from Shayne he turned off into Ninth Street. Shayne studied the cheap storefronts and hallways. Two middle-aged women holding beer cans sat on a low stoop, talking. A drunk lay curled up on newspapers in front of a dark candy store. Eddie turned again at the next corner.

"They wouldn't bring him this far."

Shayne pointed to a narrow opening between a warehouse and a blighted tenement. "What's in there?"

"Don't ask me. And I'm not going in to find out."

"I want to take a look. I'll need your headlights."

Eddie maneuvered the cab around and flicked his lights up to high beam when they pointed into the opening. It was five feet wide, littered with bottles, old tires, parts of cars and other debris. Ten feet or so in, Shayne saw what seemed to be a long heap of rags.

"If you get in any trouble," Eddie said as Shayne got out, "don't expect me to wait for you. I'm taking off."

The detective's enormous shadow filled the opening. A huge gray rat leaped at him from the shadows, scraped his leg, and was gone. His foot clanged against a rusty oil drum. As he moved closer to the pile of rags it turned into a man's body, fully dressed but without shoes. One of the feet pointed straight upward, the other was twisted at an awkward angle.

Shayne had been in the presence of violent death often enough so he knew at a glance that this was no sleeping drunk. Glass crunched under his feet. The smell of liquor was very strong. He squatted beside the body, taking his lighter out of his coat pocket. He spun the wheel and a little flare of light fell on the dead man's face.

It was Ronald Bixler.

CHAPTER 13
3:35 A.M.

SHAYNE'S EYES WERE HARD AND DANGEROUS. IF HE HAD moved faster, if he had told Bixler flatly to be satisfied with what he had cleared and not try for any more, the little man might still be alive. Shayne checked his watch to see how much time had passed since he left Bixler being sick in the bathroom. Half an hour at the most.

Bixler's face was bruised and there was a smear of drying blood beneath one eye, another bloody area on the side of his head. Shayne brushed his fingers lightly across the temple, turning the head so he could examine the wound. It was several inches long, with clearly marked edges, deep enough to have driven bone-splinters into the brain. It had been inflicted with something long and flat, with a blunted cutting edge.

He moved the lighter. The dead man's pants pockets had been turned inside out. A pale stripe around the wrist of one of the outflung arms showed where his watch had been. The redhead searched all the pockets carefully, finding nothing.

He stood up, letting the lighter flame wink out. Eddie was on the sidewalk watching. Behind him the cab's motor idled loudly.

"Senator Wall?" the driver said hoarsely as Shayne reached him.

"No. Now I need a phone."

"Is he dead?"

"Yeah," Shayne said wearily, getting into the front seat of the cab.

Eddie came around and got in beside him. "Hacking nights, you run into things. But I've got a policy—go to sleep and forget it. Why don't we let somebody else find him?"

"A phone, Eddie," Shayne repeated. "He didn't die of smoking cigarettes. Somebody killed him. This is for the cops."

"Well, sure, as a rule. But do you have any idea of the red tape you can get involved in? The company will have to know I knocked off back there for a drink. That's one example."

"Eddie," Shayne said more sharply.

"OK, but do you mind telling me who you are? I know you're a pro, but who do you work for?"

"I'm a private detective," Shayne said, "and when I come across a dead body I notify the cops. It's a habit you get into."

He checked the address of the battered tenement. Returning to Ninth Street, Eddie drove two blocks and stopped at a cheap hotel.

"I'll keep the motor running. Don't let them tie you up in a long conversation while they trace the call."

"Stop worrying, Eddie. Nobody's traced any calls since the dial system came in."

He climbed a flight of worn steps between a store and a shooting gallery. The hotel lobby was nothing but a desk and a few chairs in a corridor. An old man came out of an inner room while Shayne was leafing through a phone book hanging from a nail beside the wall phone.

"Using your phone," Shayne said.

He found fourteen precincts listed, and he chose one with a Northwest address, without being sure he was actually in that part of town. When a voice answered he said brusquely, "I'm reporting a killing. I thought it was a drunk at first, and he certainly stunk of liquor, but the guy is dead, all right. Slugged and robbed."

"What's the address?" the voice said calmly.

"Thirty-seven and a half Fortescue Street, just off Ninth. In a little open space alongside the house. It runs all the way through, a place where people throw their junk, and he's about ten feet in. I won't give you my name. I'm hanging up now."

"Wait a minute."

Shayne hung up. The old man at the desk continued to regard him impassively. Shayne nodded to him.

Returning to the cab, he told Eddie, "Drop me at Oskar's. You don't have to come in with me if you don't feel like it."

"You're an optimist, I must say," Eddie said. "What makes you think they'll let you in?"

"They'll let me in," Shayne assured him.

Eddie drove back to Larue Place, staying at the wheel after Shayne got out in front of No. 17.

"What do I owe you?" Shayne said.

"Oh, hell!" Eddie said, disgusted. He turned off the ignition and joined the redhead on the sidewalk. "It's against my principles, but they won't take just your word for it."

"Let's wait till we hear the sirens."

That took less than a minute. When the first siren began to wail Eddie went down from the sidewalk and rapped tentatively. Shayne reached past him and gave the door three hard knocks, which brought Pete in a hurry. Seeing who it was, he stepped out into the little areaway.

"Man, you guys are really asking for it."

"He's dead!" Eddie said excitably.

Another siren joined the first, coming fast. Pete moved toward the street, then checked himself.

"Who's dead? Some more Senators?"

"I have to apologize about that," Shayne said. "I told you he was a Senator, but I was wrong. His name's Bixler. He was *sent* by a Senator, and that's almost as bad. I better talk to your brother."

With a scowl on his face, Pete listened to the screams of the sirens. "I'll go in and find out."

Shayne felt a sudden hammering in back of his eyes. "Goddamn it, open that door or I'll take it to the cops and let them ask the questions."

Pete stepped back, still undecided but being worked on by the sirens. When he opened the door, Shayne pushed it out of his hand and walked through. Oskar was on his way from the bar. The sirens had reminded his customers that they were breaking the law, and the atmosphere was no longer even partially festive.

"What's going on out there?" Oskar demanded.

Pete spoke to him in an undertone. The sirens were dying as the police cars converged around Bixler.

"Take it easy," Shayne said. "They aren't interested in you yet. I told them where they could find the body. I forgot to say he was drinking in here before it happened."

"He's dead for sure?"

"If you don't want to take my word for it," Shayne said, "you know where you left him."

"Goddamn you, if this is a frame—"

Shayne interrupted. "Sure. I could have found him sleeping off his drunk and caved in his skull so I could get you to answer a few questions. Anything's possible. But I'd say the blood on his face has been drying about as long as the blood on your knuckles. We can get the cops to give us an expert opinion. A better idea might be to close up for the night and talk about it."

His customers were hurrying out. Shayne closed the door and put his back against it. Everyone was trying to talk at once. Shayne smiled good humoredly and raised his voice.

"You don't want to attract attention by piling out of here all at once. Settle your tab and leave two or three at a time."

He picked the four bar-customers who looked most sober, and took their names and addresses. They didn't like it, but they weren't backed by the management; Oskar left them to Shayne. Oskar had gone back behind the bar and was flexing his shoulders nervously. His sister, at a table for two, stared hopelessly at her blunt fingernails.

Oskar waited till all the customers had left, then burst out, "Where did you find him?"

"On Fortescue."

"On Fortescue! We left him right down the block, outside the movie."

"Not that anybody would believe you," Shayne remarked.

Oskar grunted. "What did you say your name was?"

"Michael Shayne. I think I'm working for Senator Hitchcock, but I haven't been able to get through to him recently to find out. The guy who was in here, Bixler, used to investigate for Hitchcock's committee. Everybody in the joint saw you walk out with him, and you weren't being too gentle, were you?"

"We tagged him, sure," Oscar said uneasily. "He started calling Olga names—Polack, Hunky, and like that. Nobody gets away with that stuff in here. That don't mean we killed him."

Shayne looked at the cab driver. "I appreciate your help, Eddie. Ten bucks ought to cover it. Now Oskar's going to pour you a nightcap on the house."

Eddie protested, "I thought I was going to find out what this is all about."

"You don't want to know," Shayne told him. "Bixler knew, and look where he ended up."

"Something in that," Eddie admitted.

He tossed off the whiskey Oskar poured him, said goodnight, and left. Shayne pointed to a bottle of cognac on the back bar. Oskar served him, leaving the bottle within reach. His upper lip was beaded with sweat.

"I'm not running a tearoom," he said. "I get a good class of customer, government people, and the way I keep them, I slam down fast when anybody gets noisy. This guy, we didn't land on him too hard. He passed out, more. He was carrying a load when he walked in here. All I wanted to do was jolt him, keep him walking, and he caved in on me."

He reached for a shot-glass and a bottle of sour mash and went on. "What was I supposed to do then, give taxi service? Pete and me, between us we walked him down to the corner. They have a kind of iron gate in front of the movie, we left him against that, sleeping like a baby."

"Which means," Shayne said, "that somebody was watching, probably from a car, and as soon as you were out of sight they picked him up, whacked him hard enough to make sure he wouldn't go on sleeping like a baby, and drove him a couple of blocks and dumped him. He wasn't

107

likely to be found before morning, if then. OK. You heard how it sounds. Do you think the cops are going to buy it?"

Oskar filled the shot-glass with whiskey, his hand steady. "Why not?"

"Because anything like that might get them involved with important people. I mean Senators, a big lobbyist, the president of an airplane company. You're the perfect quick solution. No toes stepped on, nothing much gets in the papers. You've got a Polish name. You run an illegal joint in a bad neighborhood. The jury wouldn't be out more than thirty seconds. That's why you've got to talk to me."

"I'm talking," Oskar said.

"And why your sister has to talk to me."

"No!" He drank the whiskey and looked down into the empty glass before setting it back on the bar. "Olga, she has nothing to do with it."

Olga exclaimed impatiently and came over to the bar.

"I have nothing to do with it? I have everything! The bad thing, Mr. Shayne, the way it started, I took the money from Bixler last year, that three thousand dollars. I knew I shouldn't. But I did. And now see."

CHAPTER 14
3:55 A.M.

"OLGA, YOU GO TO BED," OSCAR SAID. "WE'LL HANDLE THIS."
"Yes, the way you handle that little man! You only know
one thing, you and Pete. Throw him on the sidewalk, beat
him. That's all you know, beat, beat." She turned to Shayne.
"My brother Oskar, he comes out of prison. He got in fist
fight about some cheap girl, the other fellow died. He was
in three years. Now, who will believe he takes this Bixler
out and only just taps? *I* don't believe!"

Oskar raised his hand. "Olga, but the memory of our
mother, I'm telling you—"

Olga sniffed. "It was all right when I took his money.
That was fine. Now he wants to talk to me, you take him
out and kill him."

Her other brother said warmly, "I was there, for Christ's
sake! I put a newspaper under his head! Oskar didn't kill
him and I didn't kill him."

Shayne put in, "Will everybody please stop talking?
Personally I think you're telling the truth, Szep. But if your
own sister won't believe you, don't be too surprised if a
jury won't. We've got a little time before they pick you up.
Are you with me so far?"

"I better get in the car and start moving, huh?"

"Not just yet. There's no identification on the body. No
shoes. He's covered with dirt and blood. He looks like a
bum and smells like a bum, and they won't bother about him
much until they take his prints in the morning. They may
not hurry with that, but they're sure to know who he is by
noon. I'm beginning to get a few faint ideas, but I need some
cooperation, in fact all the cooperation I can get. You can
help, Olga. Will you try to remember exactly what Bixler
said when he came in?"

She moved a stool out from the bar and sat down, her chin on one hand. "Do we have champagne, and will I drink some with him. I said my brothers don't allow. Then he said why do I go away from town last year. I said I was scared. He said did anybody else ever ask me about the diary. Then Oskar came over."

"What did he pay you the three thousand bucks for, a look at Mrs. Masterson's diary?"

Olga nodded. "That was her name then."

"What do you mean—she married again?"

"Uh-huh, to that Senator, I forget his name."

"Redpath?" Shayne said sharply.

"That's right, Redpath. I saw her picture in the paper."

Shayne tapped his fingers on the bar and fitted another piece on the puzzle into place. "How long did you work for her?"

"How long, Oskar? Maybe a year. Good pay, but she had so many dinners. Eighteen, twenty people. They never sat down before eight-thirty, it was twelve when you finished the dishes. An hour to go home. Back at eight the next morning. I said to her once, I better sleep at her house the nights she has a party. There's maid's room. She said no. I know why—then I might find out who came back to sleep with her after everybody went home."

"I didn't want Olga to take that job," Oskar said, "but try telling Olga."

"Why did she fire you?" Shayne asked.

"She said I didn't keep the house clean. Those floors sparkled! The silver, always A-one condition. The bathrooms—perfect." She gave an indignant sniff. "One night I get home to my house and forget the key. I must go all the way back in a taxicab, or sleep on the sidewalk. You think I try to find out who she has in her bedroom? She can have fifty men if she wants to. I don't care. I go in by the back door. I know where I leave the key, on the drainboard by the sink. And Mrs. Masterson comes stamping downstairs very mad, in her bathrobe. Oh, she was so mad. What am I doing, spying on her? Some people. She did have a man up there, I see his hat in the hall, one of those army hats."

Shayne swung around. "Do you remember what color braid? What kind of insignia?"

"What kind of what?"

Oskar explained in Polish, and Olga said, "Some big bird, like an eagle?"

Shayne smiled for the first time since finding Bixler's body. "Now how about the diary?"

Olga said bitterly, "I wish I never saw that diary."

Oskar filled Shayne's glass and poured another shot for himself. "What did you do that was so bad, Olga? He said they were crooks, they were robbing the government, and you had to help so he could stop it."

"Oh, yes, and I helped him. I turned into a thief myself."

"You didn't steal it, you borrowed it! I've told you time and again."

"Steal it, they know it's gone. Borrow it and put it back, maybe they don't even know it happened. That's worse."

Shayne was pulling at his earlobe. "Bixler told me he didn't go through with it."

Olga laughed without humor. "He lied, Mr. Shayne."

"How did you work it?"

"This diary," she said, "she kept it locked in a box on the back of a shelf in the bedroom closet. If she didn't want me to know where she puts the key to the box, the other little key to the diary, she should change her own towels and vacuum-clean and straighten up and make her own beds. In one year, the maid finds out little things. When I tell Bixler I know about the keys, oh, he goes crazy. This was after she fired me, and I had to give her back my key to the house. He got another key for me. He told me what I must do. One day we practiced, to be sure there was time for everything. The day after when she went out to lunch—he knew she was going out to lunch, he had everything worked out—he called the house. The new maid answers, he says it's the furnace company, go down and get the number off the furnace. There was no number! That was his business, to know how to do those things. So the maid is looking for it in the basement, I unlock the back door very very quietly and walk up to the bedroom, get the keys

111

from the desk, open the box, unlock the diary, put the keys back, the box back, hurry downstairs—one minute, no more."

"Did you look in the diary?"

"I had no time. Everything was all hurry, hurry."

"Olga, you know you looked in it. You're human."

"I opened it, but it was in this tiny writing, you'd need hours to read one sentence. Every day she put down names for lunch, names for dinner, and numbers, like two hundred dollars, five hundred dollars."

"You couldn't make out any of the names?"

"You try reading something that little in a taxi sometime. Bouncing around. And I was *scared*. I couldn't keep my mind on it. I put it in a locker at the Greyhound depot. I went back and watched the house to be sure she didn't come home early. One hour later, back to the depot, get the diary. The three thousand dollars was in an envelope. We spent it to air-condition this place for Oskar, the down payment on the mortgage."

"Wait a minute. How did Bixler get the key to the locker after you left the diary in it?"

"That part I didn't tell. He sent me the key in the mail the day before. He had another, see? Then he called the maid and talked to her on the phone in the kitchen and I walked in the front door, as bold as you please. All over. Then he said I should move to another house and be careful. I thought, if he says be careful, I'll be extra careful, so I went to my other brother and sister-in-law in the Bronx, New York. I stayed four months."

Shayne said slowly, "Are you sure it was Bixler who arranged all this?"

She looked at him as though he had challenged some basic religious belief. "He said he was Bixler, Ronald Bixler."

"OK," Shayne said. "This sounds simple because it worked, but it was really pretty complicated. From the depot he'd have to take the diary to an office, and back to the depot. Even with a high-speed copier, say a late-model

Zerox, the timing would have to be close. How did he work it all out with you, on the phone?"

She shook her head. "No, I saw him. He came to my house once, once I met him in a cafeteria. After that it was on the phone. The keys, I told you, in the mail. He fixed it so the day it happened nobody saw us together. He said there was dangerous, danger. I was the one he was thinking about, so I wouldn't go to jail for stealing when all I did was borrow for two hours. He didn't have to tell *me* to be careful. I was careful, believe me."

Oskar said, "Notice that only one person ran any risks, and it was Olga? What did *he* do besides get a couple of keys made and call the house? If anybody had asked me, which they didn't, I'd say don't settle for a measly three grand. That's a three- to ten-year rap for burglary right there. To tell the truth, it's the main reason I clipped him tonight. That always griped me."

"The thing that bothers me," Shayne said, "is where did he get his hands on three thousand bucks?"

They looked at him blankly. He explained, "That's a lot of cash in one lump for anybody at his level."

Pete said scornfully, "That's how much you know. You should see the roll he was flashing tonight."

"I'm not talking about tonight," Shayne said. "Tonight he had hundreds sticking out of his ears. You must know by now that this thing was never legitimate. Whoever got hold of the diary has been using it for blackmail. A year ago Bixler was trying to live on his salary, and just getting by. If he was the one who laid out that three thousand, it means somebody else was bankrolling him. And maybe they didn't bother to use him at all. Think about it."

Olga seemed disturbed and upset. "I could tell his voice on the phone! That way he said 's,' like he sort of stuttered."

"That wouldn't be hard to imitate." He rapped abruptly on the bar. "All right, Pete, let's see what you took off him."

Pete stepped backward, a denial forming on his lips. "So help me God—"

Ignoring him, Shayne looked at his older brother. "What

do they use for executions in Washington, the gas chamber? If I knew what he had in his wallet, it might help."

Oskar moved along the bar toward Pete and said dangerously, "Is that what you did when you went back to put a newspaper under his head?"

"No!"

When Oskar continued to advance he said hastily, "OK! OK! I'll give it to the Red Cross or somebody. What was I supposed to do, leave him lying there, with all that dough in his pocket, for the first wino who came along? What kind of sense would it make?"

"What a family," Olga said.

"Do what Shayne says," Oskar told him. "Dump it out on the stick, all of it."

Swearing, Pete emptied his pants pockets in front of Shayne: a wallet, keys, change, a fountain pen, a wristwatch. Shayne counted the money. It came to over nine hundred dollars. Carrying that much cash in this neighborhood, and letting it be seen, had been a good way to invite a knock on the head. Shayne emptied the card pockets of the wallet. The dead man had belonged to the Diners' Club, Carte Blanche, the American Legion, the American Rifle Association, Sigma Alpha Epsilon, the Elks. The membership cards gave him an identity that he had seemed to lack in real life. There were a number of girls' names and phone numbers, and he had carried a color photograph of an older woman, probably his mother.

"Any of that mean anything?" Oskar asked anxiously.

Only one thing appeared to be current. It was a note scribbled on ruled paper and stuck into the money compartment: "Week of June 25—check safe deposit boxes, all Washington banks."

"Can you give me the date when you took the diary?" Shayne asked Olga. "I know it was last year, but when last year?"

"In the spring," she said doubtfully. "May, June?"

"End of June," Oskar said. "I was only out of the can a month."

Shayne put Bixler's watch on his right wrist. Everything

else he stuffed back in the wallet and snapped a heavy rubber band around it.

"This goes to the cops tomorrow noon, along with the names of the four witnesses who saw you bounce him. That gives us—" he consulted his own watch—"seven and a half hours."

"Man, anything we can do—" Oskar said.

"I might think of something," Shayne said dryly. "This has all been pretty one-sided so far."

"Anything," Oskar repeated, planting both hands on the bar and looking directly at Shayne. "I mean it."

USING THE PHONE BEHIND THE BAR, SHAYNE DIALED THE
Hotel St. Albans, where he had checked in the previous
afternoon.

"Michael Shayne, please. Room 1232."

Oskar Szep looked around in surprise. "Didn't you say
that's your name?"

Shayne silenced him with a wave. The switchboard girl
soon told him there was no answer from that room. He
said to keep ringing. Finally Shayne heard a click and a
man's voice said gruffly, as though surfacing out of a heavy
sleep, " 'Lo."

"Rebman?" Shayne said sharply, his mouth several inches
from the phone.

"Yes," the voice said more alertly. "Shayne hasn't come
back yet. The way it begins to look, he's sleeping out. But
all his stuff is still here, and there's a chance he may be in
to shave before breakfast. We'll be ready for him, don't
worry."

"There's been a change of plans," Shayne said in his ordinary tone. "Forget about Shayne. Everything's starting to
fall apart. Get the hell to the airport and catch the first
plane out."

There was a pause, and Rebman said, "Is that you,
Shamus?"

The redhead laughed. "You boys always do the obvious
thing. Waiting in my hotel room, for God's sake! I hate to
think how much it cost you to get in."

"It didn't cost too much," Rebman said. "This is the
second time you've suckered me. There won't be a third.
I've got new instructions, and they don't leave me any
leeway. The money offers are out. If you want to go home,

fine, nobody'll come after you. But leave your suitcase here and send for it. Am I making myself clear?"

"Sure. Now will you give your boss a message? Tell Mr. Manners he's going to be under a different kind of pressure starting tomorrow morning. Maybe he's the one who ought to go home. Bribery and blackmail don't seem to mean anything any more—it's like drinking hard liquor during Prohibition. Murder's something else. Questions about a murder always have that little extra bit of steam."

"Who's been murdered?"

"If you don't know, Rebman, I think I'll let you find out for yourself. Give him the message."

Shayne hung up abruptly.

"Say," Pete said as Shayne turned, "I just thought of something. One of our regulars came in right after Bixler, Billy, we call him. Like he was plastered, but maybe he saw if the guy came in a cab, or what. He lives down the street, and what I'm going to do, I'm going to wake him up and ask him."

He went out at a quick walk. Shayne took his glass and the cognac bottle to a table and asked Olga to sit down with him.

"Let's go through the whole thing again, starting with the first time Bixler got in touch with you. What he said, what you said, the whole thing."

She lowered her voice so her brother, who had stayed at the bar, wouldn't hear her. "You really think they left him in front of the movie? And somebody else came along and killed him?"

"He was hit when he was already out," Shayne said. "I don't know what with—a tire iron or the blunt end of a railroad spike. It was a funny-shaped wound. Does that sound like Pete and Oskar?"

"No-o. In a fight. Not if he's lying there sleeping."

"OK, Olga, you and Bixler. Take your time."

He listened attentively, occasionally asking a quiet question. Pete burst in ten minutes later.

"A black and white hardtop!" he announced. "How do you like that?"

"Yeah, but *Billy*," his brother said skeptically. "He'd make some witness."

"He won't get as far as court," Pete admitted. "He'll forget about it in the morning. But it's a start, ain't it? I could hardly make out what he was saying, half the time. He couldn't find his teeth. The only reason he remembers— the guy stepped on his toes. When he got out of the car, and he didn't say he was sorry. Billy's still steaming."

"Are you sure he knew who you meant?" Oskar said.

"Sure I'm sure. The guy we threw out. He remembers the car because he was going to pound in the fender. He looked around and picked up the first thing he saw—an old broken piece of a torsion rod, and he was all set to do it when he saw there was somebody sitting in the car. That scared him, and he threw the rod away and came in for a drink. Black and white hardtop, a good car, good shape. That's all I could get out of him, and I was shaking him half the time."

Shayne pulled hard at his earlobe. He had seen a black car with a white top somewhere recently, but he couldn't remember where. If he didn't push it too hard it would come to him.

Pete said, "Something else I been thinking about—that dough."

"What dough?" Shayne said.

"In the wallet. Who'd know the difference if we cut it up in three shares?"

"If you didn't take it in the first place," his sister said angrily, "and left it for somebody else, they'd be in this trouble, not you. Mr. Shayne talked me out of thinking you did it. What are you trying to do, talk me back in? Now beat it. I'm telling Mr. Shayne."

For the next half-hour she went on talking disjointedly, going over and over each episode until Shayne was sure she had told him all she could remember. Something below the surface was working at him. When he finished the bottle, Oskar brought another. Pete, two tables away, smoked cigarette after cigarette. Oskar stayed at the bar, rarely taking his eyes off Shayne. Only the cognac kept the redhead awake. He was both tense and relaxed. His eyes glazed, his mind began to drift, and suddenly something Olga said broke through to him.

"—telling the truth," she said, and Shayne came back so suddenly that his hand jerked and the glass fell from his fingers.

Olga stopped talking and watched him. Wide awake and back in action, he went to the phone. If Bixler had been telling the truth about the diary episode, maybe Maggie Smith had been telling the truth about her friendship with Hitchcock. There was only one Margaret Smith in the phone book. He dialed that number.

It rang a long time, and Maggie's hello was stifled and unclear.

"Wake up, Mrs. Smith," Shayne said briskly. "This is Michael Shayne."

"Who?"

"*Shayne*. The crude son of a bitch who's been trying to break up your romance with Senator Hitchcock. Are you awake?"

"Michael Shayne? Do you know what time it is?"

"It's five-ten, and I thought I'd better tell you that the guy who told me about your Caribbean cruise has been murdered."

"Murdered!"

"Yeah. He was already unconscious. Somebody broke his head open with a torsion rod, if you know what that is, and left him on a dump for the rats."

"Well, damn you, that wakes me up. Is this a joke?"

"No, Mrs. Smith. His name was Bixler, and I don't really think you killed him. Unless you drive a black and white hardtop?"

"I drive a Volkswagen, and I wouldn't know a hardtop if I saw one. Listen here, Mr. Shayne—"

"Didn't we decide at one point you were going to call me Mike?"

"Are you drunk, by any chance?"

"Slightly, and I'm tired. Is anybody with you?"

She drew in her breath sharply and slammed down the phone.

Shayne looked up the number and dialed it again. She let it ring as long as she could stand it, then picked it up and said angrily, "You're a grown man, try to act like one. What did I do to bring this on?"

"I'm sorry. I didn't know how that was going to sound. To put it another way, would it be all right if I come over? Don't hang up! All of a sudden it's occurred to me that maybe you've been telling the truth."

He wasn't sure she was still on the line until she said suspiciously, "Which of your various accusations are you withdrawing?"

"All of them. I don't think you're working for Sam Toby. I don't think you knew he set up that dinner where you met Hitchcock. I don't think you've been trying to blackmail anybody. This puts things in a different light. I really think you've been used by some pretty crummy people."

"I did go to the Caribbean with that Department of Labor man," she said after a moment.

"That's long in the past. There's something I want you to do for me, Maggie. Can I come over?"

"Mike, I don't know! I may not have much of a reputation, but I'd like to keep what little I have. Not to mention the fact that I don't *know* you."

"Wait a minute. Even if I had any such ideas, which I didn't before you brought it up—"

"Before *I* brought it up!"

Shayne continued, beginning to grin, "We've got too much else to cover. Maybe you'll invite me to breakfast."

"Breakfast isn't entirely impossible," she said doubtfully, "but—"

"I'll be there in fifteen minutes," he said, and hung up before she could point out that she hadn't yet decided to invite him. He underlined her address in the phone book and tore out the page.

"Are you going to need us?" Oskar said.

"I think so," Shayne said, his mind racing. "There are

some Texans in town, and they keep telling me what they're going to do to me the next time they see me. First I'm going to wake up a few more people."

He dialed the home phone of Senator William P. Redpath. Someone cut off the ring almost before it started, but all Shayne could hear was the sound of heavy breathing.

"Hello!" he shouted. He whistled into the phone. "Hello! Mrs. Redpath?"

"Hello," a man's voice said fuzzily.

"Sorry to be calling you at this hour," Shayne said loudly, "but will you get Mrs. Redpath to the phone?"

"Who's this?" the voice said more distinctly.

"My name is Shayne. If this is Senator Redpath, your wife knows me. I want to ask her about a woman named Olga Szep who used to work for her before she married you."

He winked at Olga reassuringly. There was silence at the other end of the line for a long moment.

"Let me have your name again."

"Shayne. I've been working all night on the Sam Toby investigation. Your wife's name keeps cropping up, sometimes as Mrs. Redpath and sometimes as Mrs. Masterson."

Adelle Redpath's voice exploded in Shayne's ear. "What a ghastly hour! Precisely what do you mean by this, Mr. Shayne?"

"I've already told your husband I was sorry," Shayne said. "Don't shout. I've had a bad night. I thought you'd want to know what happened to your diary."

Probably she had been in tight places before, and she didn't gasp or cry out, but merely said cautiously, "I've lost touch with Olga in the past year."

"Does that mean your husband doesn't know you used to keep a diary?"

"Not yet. And I hope that continues."

"OK. I expect you know that it was copied, on or about June 25th last year. It's my guess that only one copy exists. There's a chance I can get hold of it. If I do, I'll turn it over to you without reading it, in return for a small amount of cooperation from you and your husband."

"And you're a private detective?"

"You'll have to take it on faith," Shayne snapped. "I want to talk to Senator Redpath the first thing in the morning, and I want you to arrange it for me. Between now and then I think you have to tell him the full story."

"Why?"

"The big reason is that an investigator who helped organize the theft of your diary was murdered tonight."

"What did you say?" she said quickly.

"You heard me. The body hasn't been identified yet. We may have until noon. If it hasn't been cleared up by then, the whole thing has to come out. That means names, dates and prices."

"My God. How do you figure in this?"

"People have been making me look dumb ever since I got to town, Mrs. Redpath, I'm sorry to say including you. I can't be expected to like it, and right here is where it stops. Now ask your husband where would be a good place to meet."

"Call me back. I want to think it over first."

"You can think faster than that. I'm in a hurry."

She covered the mouthpiece. Oskar brought Shayne a new drink, and he sipped it while she convinced her husband.

"There's a room on the Senate side of the Capitol, on the gallery level, G 251," she said curtly. "At ten."

Shayne agreed. After hanging up he sat looking down into his cognac and waiting for the name of the National Aviation lobbyist to come to him. Someone had mentioned it in passing, and he hadn't supposed he would ever need to know it. But it was there. It rose to the surface after a moment—Henry Clark. There were four Henry Clarks listed, and Shayne dialled the one that had two office phones and one residence. This time the voice that answered was crisp and alert.

"Yes?"

"Does the name Shayne ring any bell with you?"

"Yes, indeed. I heard you were in town."

"Would you know what I was talking about if I said that

Senator Hitchcock won't be seeing anything more of Mrs. Smith?"

"I'd have a faint idea," Clark said. "And as an admirer of Senator Hitchcock, I'm happy to hear it. That was fast. Will you be going back in the morning?"

"I doubt it. Too many other things have happened. Mr. Clark, what's the most your company hopes to get out of this Toby investigation? What stakes are you playing for?"

Clark considered. "We're walking a rather fine line there, Shayne. If the hearings produce evidence of some transaction that is so raw and extreme that Manners can't be allowed to keep the contract, it will fall in my client's lap. No one would like that. The program's already nine months behind and any shift would mean a further delay. Whatever you care to say about Hugh Manners, he's an excellent production man. We don't want the Pentagon really mad at us. It's all right to rock the boat, but not to turn it over."

"I'm trying to find out what you do want."

"I don't like to talk about it on the phone. Can we meet for breakfast?"

"I have a date for breakfast, and after that I'll be busy. If somebody's bugging us, that's just too bad. I'm told you've been working closely with Senator Wall. I could be wrong, but I'd say that the odds are about five to one that he's changed sides."

"I'd be interested to know what makes you say that. Quite frankly, it would hurt."

"I haven't worked it all out yet. You still haven't told me what National wants to get out of it."

"We'd like to recover our expenses in the contract competition, a matter of some ten million dollars. We want part of the subcontract for the airframe assembly, to keep one of our key plants in operation. And we want an informal assurance that our bid on the new Navy fighter program will be given, oh, a two- or three-point edge because of the shellacking we took on this last one, through no fault of our own. Those three things."

"Are they worth fifty thousand bucks?"

"You really have to understand, Mr. Shayne—"

"I know, you don't want to talk about money on the phone. But I'll want a written agreement, and if that price sounds right, be in the rotunda of the Capitol at ten-twenty. Wipe your forehead with a handkerchief now and then so I'll recognize you."

"You've certainly given me something to think about, Mr. Shayne."

"And I need some information I can't get myself. I want to know who rented safe-deposit boxes in the principal Washington banks the week of June 25th last year. Is that possible?"

"If it's important. I doubt if I could have it by ten-twenty."

"Bring as many of them as you can. I may be a little late."

CHAPTER 16
5:30 A.M.

MAGGIE SMITH'S HOUSE WAS ONE OF A ROW NOT FAR FROM her theatre, on a narrow street. Shayne made a note to duck when he went through the front door. The Szep brothers, who had followed in a Chevy pick-up, parked several blocks away, where the truck would be less conspicuous, and came back to wait in Shayne's Ford. Shayne gave them descriptions of Stevens, Rebman, and the Mexican gunman who had accompanied Stevens. He didn't expect them to look for him here, but they had surprised him before.

The sky was beginning to lighten in the east. Maggie Smith opened the door almost as soon as Shayne let go of the antique brass knocker. She was wearing slacks, high-heeled gold sandals, and a sleeveless green blouse, and her immediate effect on the redheaded detective was to make him forget to duck. As he stepped inside he grazed the top of his head on the lintel.

"I should have warned you," she said. "These are famous houses, and thousands of tourists come by to gawk at them every day, but they're *small*. Oh Mike!" Closing the door, she came in against him for an instant. "You're so big and solid and comforting. I've been humming to myself ever since I got up. You've decided to believe me!"

"I tried believing everybody else first."

"I don't care! So long as you came around to believing me in the end. Go through to the kitchen. I'm in the middle of making breakfast."

Shayne followed her down a narrow hall, papered in a striped pattern, with a stepped row of oval miniatures on the wall. The kitchen was large and modern. It was filled with pleasant smells. Coffee was filtering on the stove. A dozen strips of bacon were laid out to drain on paper towels and a bowl of uncooked scrambled eggs was ready to be poured into the pan. Something was underway in a wall oven.

"The muffins have ten more minutes. Coffee's almost ready. The eggs—I hope you like eggs—"

"I like eggs," Shayne said.

"Sit down." She pointed him toward a big table, already prepared for two. "I know it would be more polite to wait till you've eaten something, but Mike, what happened? The last time I saw you, you certainly gave no signs of disagreeing with Trina Hitchcock. What made you change your mind?"

Shayne stuck a cigarette in the corner of his mouth. "A funny thing happened. I talked to Hugh Manners, and he claimed he'd never heard a thing about it. I happened to have something to bargain with, and I told him to get Toby on the phone and call it off. And he got Toby on the phone, and Toby called it off."

She gave him a worried look. "You mean Toby himself admitted—"

"Yeah, and not only that. I've got it in Manners' writing. He gave me a letter to Hitchcock. You can read it if you want to. The idea was that I wouldn't use it unless you gave me more trouble. Manners says he's just found out that you and Toby have been setting up Hitchcock for a dirty photograph. It's not that specific, but Hitchcock would understand what he's getting at. And then Manners says he's sorry and tells Hitchcock not to worry—it's all off."

"He *signed* that? Why would he sign such a lie?"

"Didn't know it was a lie," Shayne said, the sharp outlines of everything in the kitchen beginning to fuzz over and blur. "Believed me and Toby. You said one thing, Toby said another. I tried believing Toby, made no sense. Because all a fake. Tried believing you, made sense."

He had been able to stay awake and clear-headed in a hard, uncomfortable chair in Oskar's after-hours bar, but here in the airy kitchen, filled as it was with pleasant cooking smells, he could feel himself going.

"Don't fall *asleep!*" Maggie said urgently. "Mike, I have to know! What do you mean, all a fake?"

Shayne snapped out of it, giving his head a short shake. "How's the coffee coming?"

"One more minute. What could Toby hope to gain by telling Manners something he knew wasn't true? Aren't they working together?"

"Toby's been conning everybody, Manners too. He had to."

As Shayne's eyes began to close again Maggie hurriedly splashed some too-strong coffee into a cup and put it in front of him. The fumes brought him back for a moment, but getting the cup to his mouth, or his mouth to the cup, seemed to be beyond him. He blinked hard, then his eyelids relaxed and everything began to swirl.

She shook his shoulder. "Damn you, Michael Shayne! You can't say something cryptic like that, and dodge out of it by going to sleep. Drink your coffee."

He could hear her, but her voice seemed to come at him from a great distance, rising and falling as though being blown about by a strong wind. He managed to take the coffee cup in both hands. He lowered his face toward it, meeting it halfway. It was scalding hot. The first mouthful burned its way down and his head cleared.

"There's no time to sleep!" he said. "I've got to explain something. I think I know what happened but I can't prove it. I need your help."

"What can't you prove, that Toby was lying?"

"No, no. That—"

The cup began to tilt. He watched, powerless to stop what he saw happening. Maggie took it out of his hand and put it back on the table.

"All right," she said more philosophically. "I can see you're determined. You woke me up in the middle of the night, and now you can't stay awake yourself to tell me why. If you think I'm going to carry you upstairs, you're very much mistaken."

"I just need a minute," Shayne mumbled. "Some more coffee."

"It's too hot to drink, and you won't still be awake when it cools off. Stand up."

He shook his head, frowning. "Got to tell you something. It wasn't Toby's idea."

She pulled at him gently, and he toppled sideward, knowing that if he went to sleep now the machinery he was caught up in would go faster and faster until it crashed into something and broke apart. Maggie guided him toward the living room. He heard a low hum from an electric clock on the wall and saw the sweep second hand revolving slowly. He was past before he was able to decipher the time.

He tried again. "Toby's the hired man. He wasn't—"

"No, Mike," she said when he didn't go on. "He definitely wasn't. You can finish that sentence after you wake up."

"I can't go to sleep!" he exclaimed, finding himself lying on a broad sofa, with no memory of having crossed the living room. "You don't understand."

"You can say that again," Maggie said, untying his shoe laces. "And the reason I'm taking off your shoes is not because I want you to be comfortable, but because I don't want my sofa to get dirty. When do you want me to wake you up?"

"I can't go to sleep," Shayne insisted.

He could hear his own voice, but that was all, and it went on echoing for a long time. Damn right he couldn't go to sleep. He had to meet Senator Redpath at the Capitol at ten, and he had a lot of persuading to do first. Ten was the absolute deadline. Ten o'clock.

CHAPTER 17
10:00 A.M.

WHEN HE AWOKE HE KNEW IMMEDIATELY WHERE HE WAS. He heard the low hum of the electric clock, and brought his hand up to look at his watch. It said ten o'clock on the button, and while that was registering, an announcer's voice from a radio somewhere said cheerfully that it was already fifteen seconds past the hour.

"Maggie!" he yelled.

She ran in from the kitchen as he erupted off the sofa. "Mike! I thought you'd stay in that coma another twenty-four hours. Coffee coming right up."

"No time for coffee." He grabbed his shoes. "Come on, I'll explain as we go."

"Mike, I can't go anywhere dressed like this."

"Sure you can, you look great," he said, without looking at her, and hauled her to the front door. "The first thing you have to understand is that everything is the opposite of the way it seemed."

"I've got to turn off the stove! Go on, I'll catch up."

She ran to the kitchen swiftly. He remembered to duck as he went out the front door. Oskar Szep, seeing him striding down the brick walk carrying his shoes, leaped out of the Ford.

"I wondered what this doll *did* to you. It's after ten."

"One minute after," Shayne said. "Get the pick-up and let's go."

Maggie ran out of the house while Shayne was pulling on his shoes. As soon as the Chevy swung around the corner Shayne put the Ford in gear and shot away.

"You need something to eat," Maggie said. "I brought you a muffin."

"A *muffin!*" Shayne said. "Now listen carefully. I figured

129

I'd need about three hours to bring you up to date and talk you into doing me a favor. Now I have ten minutes, and I sure as hell can't do it with my mouth full. I want to end up at the Capitol, so if I make a wrong turn, correct me. In a nutshell. Everybody thinks this started when Hugh Manners hired Toby to get him a contract to build an airplane. It started before that, around June 25th last year, with a stolen diary."

She murmured occasionally to show she was listening, and didn't waste any of his time by making him repeat anything. As he turned past the Grant Memorial into the circle leading up to the Capitol, he said, "But how the hell am I going to prove any of that? Everybody's been too cagey. There's only one way I can see. You used to be an actress. What about doing some ad-libbing for me? So long as you understand the general outlines—"

"Which I still don't."

"I'll keep driving around and around until you do. The thing to remember is that we've got an advantage right now, and we'll lose it the minute they identify Bixler. We've got to cut a few corners and jolt people, get them to do something they wouldn't do after thinking it over."

"You'll have a hard time jolting Senator Wall. He'll just say, 'Excuse me, I have to talk to my lawyer.'"

"Then we'll put on some more pressure. Where do Senators park their cars?"

"Behind the Senate Office Building. No, that way."

Shayne followed her directions, which took him along First Street between two large official-looking buildings into a paved court. Only about half the slots reserved for Senators were being used. The slot marked "Senator Thomas Wall" was filled by a recent-model Mercury, a hardtop with a white top and a black body.

"That's what I thought," Shayne said with satisfaction.

He reversed, passing his amateur bodyguards in the Chevy pick-up, and returned to the Capitol. When he got out Maggie slid over to take the wheel.

"You do look great in those slacks," he said, really looking at her, "but if you'll feel better in a dress, you have twenty minutes. Better make it fifteen. Wait."

He went to the other side of the car and opened the front door.

"You're getting the muffin?" she said approvingly. "You really do need something."

"I do," he said fervently, and took out the blended whiskey Hugh Manners had pressed on him the night before, hoping he would use it to put himself to sleep. Unscrewing the top, he took a long pull. As he lowered the bottle he found himself being watched solemnly by three women and a row of little girls. All, including the women, were in Girl Scout uniforms.

"I missed breakfast," he explained.

Maggie laughed as he tossed the bottle back in the car. Oskar was getting out of the Chevy. The Girl Scouts opened for Shayne, and he took the shallow steps two at a time. Oskar followed, entering the rotunda while Shayne was asking the guard at the door for directions.

"Get a guidebook or something so you won't stick out so damn much," Shayne told Oskar, overtaking him. "And tell Pete to roll down his sleeves to hide those damn tattoos."

"Jesus, Mike, what if the cops have found out who Bixler is by now? Are we making any headway?"

"Relax, Oskar. Try to look like a tourist."

Shayne found the room in which Senator Redpath had arranged to meet him. The door was unlocked and he went in without knocking.

It was a narrow conference room, with a dozen or so chairs around a long oval table. A man at the window swung around as Shayne entered. He was tall, heavily built, with jowly features, which probably still looked statesmanlike in a campaign photograph.

"You're Shayne?"

It was close to an accusation. His voice was clear and resonant. Turned on its full power, Shayne was sure it could reach the last row in a large hall with no help from a microphone.

"I'm behind schedule," Shayne said. "Let's skip the preliminaries. Did Mrs. Redpath explain her problem?"

Senator Redpath moved out a chair and sat down. He looked at Shayne sharply, reminding the detective that one of the things he had been planning to do at Maggie Smith's was wash and shave.

"I need some sort of bonafides before I can talk to you freely," Redpath said. "Adelle thinks you're working for Hitchcock."

"As of this minute," Shayne said honestly, "I'm not working for anybody. I was hired by Trina Hitchcock, but I think the money for the fee came from National Aviation, through Henry Clark. For obvious reasons, National didn't want Toby to get a blackmail handle to use on Hitchcock. I don't have time to be anything but blunt, Senator. I'm assuming that your wife's diary was the lever that got this whole thing moving. Toby could use it against your wife and various other people whose names were mentioned in it. Apparently there were enough of those to put over the Manners contract. Clark tells me it's too late to revoke that now. He'll settle for a couple of concessions, and an assurance that the diary won't be used when Manners comes back to Washington looking for more business. If I can destroy it or turn it over to you, I'll collect a fee of fifty thousand clams. I think that puts us on the same side of the fence. But if you wait to check every statement I've just made—"

Senator Redpath shifted his weight abruptly. "I'll accept that, Shayne. What do you want to know from me?"

"Who approached you about backing Manners?"

The Senator began preparing a long cigar. He hesitated, then spoke decisively. "My wife, of course, on Toby's behalf."

"Did he give her any proof that he'd got hold of her diary, or had access to it?"

"He showed her several snippets cut from a photostatic copy. I wasn't aware that any such document existed until this morning. She merely asked me to look into the Manners bid to see if I could back it, and she said it was important to her. I knew she had been associated with Toby. I assumed there was something about that association which could be misinterpreted, and he had reminded her of that. I asked only one question, whether this would be the final claim he would lay on her. Her answer was yes. Our marriage was a calculated risk on my part, Shayne. On the whole I considered it successful. She manages my household well. She is an excellent hostess, a marvelous campaigner. In last fall's election I credit her with picking up between fifteen and twenty thousand votes. I won by eight thousand."

Shayne kept his feelings about all this to himself. "And those fifteen to twenty thousand voters wouldn't understand if her Toby connection made the back-home papers."

"That describes the situation. However, if my investigation of Manners' bid hadn't convinced me that he would build the best plane, I would never have had any part in it."

"Was an Air Force colonel involved?"

Redpath twirled his cigar until it was burning evenly. "That would be Colonel Oulihan, executive aide to the Source Selection Board."

"What's that?"

"An ad hoc committee which evaluated the test results and made recommendations, through channels, to the various commands."

"How much weight does a colonel pull on something like that?"

"He can pull quite a bit, depending on the caliber of his chairman. Oulihan's, a major general, doesn't happen to be one of the most brilliant officers in the armed services." He looked at his cigar reflectively. "So *Oulihan* was in on this. That explains why Manners knew the exact details of the opposing bids. Not only that, he seemed to have an uncanny grasp of the basis on which the bids were being judged."

"I don't get that."

"Every proposal's a compromise," Redpath explained. "If you add too much speed you may have to cut down on your cruising range. You have to balance performance against logistics, both against costs. Most companies make a practice of coming in with a hungry bid, planning to get it back on cost overruns, and it's known that the Secretary disapproves. But how strongly does he disapprove? And so on. An ally on the Source Selection Board would make all the difference between guessing right in such matters and guessing wrong." He added casually, "Is Oulihan one of the cast of characters in Adelle's diary?"

"Hell, I don't know," Shayne said irritably.

"You'll want to know how much I had to do with Manners' success. I spent several hours at the White House, an afternoon at the Pentagon. I made four phone calls, I wrote one letter, I introduced Manners' chief engineer to a brigadier general. I kept a log of these activities, which were actually fairly routine. I did one other thing which I didn't record. I occasionally play golf with one of the Joint Chiefs. One afternoon I remarked that I hoped Manners would get the contract. That may sound innocuous enough, but I make it a habit never to intervene with the military except in matters of extreme importance. I believe he got the message. He has to come before the Senate Finance Committee for his appropriation, and as you may know, my views carry some weight on that committee."

"OK," Shayne said. "If I told you that Senator Wall stole your wife's diary and organized this whole thing, what would you say?"

The Senator took his cigar out of his mouth in surprise. "I'd say you're out of your mind. He's National's man."

"Do you know that for a fact?"

"Three companies, closely linked to National, contributed to his campaign fund in the last election. Contributed heavily. I would also guess that he has the promise of an executive position in the company after he leaves the Senate. He identifies with their interests, and always has. There is absolutely no question about that."

"I want to ask him a few questions, just the same. I'd like to have you along as a referee. Can you get Hitchcock to call a recess?"

"Easily." As he looked at Shayne, the detective saw a

faint flicker of worry in his cold eyes. "Do you think there's a chance of wiping this damned diary out of existence?"

"We can sure as hell try. We'd better not leave together. Where's the hearing being held?"

"Second floor of the new office building." He got up heavily. "Shayne."

"Yeah?"

Looking at the oil paintings on the wall as though he was noticing them for the first time, he said, "I mentioned Adelle's participation in my last campaign so I wouldn't seem like a fool for marrying her. I also happen to—love her very much. She's a thoroughly captivating woman. If you can get this incubus off our backs, send me a bill. You'll have my check in the return mail."

He looked at Shayne with a return of his usual manner. "But how you expect to accomplish it by flinging wild charges at Tom Wall, I fail to see."

Shayne grinned. "You never know, do you?"

CHAPTER 18
10:35 A.M.

FROM THE RAILED BALCONY AROUND THE ROTUNDA, SHAYNE spotted Henry Clark, the National Aviation lobbyist, on the paved floor below, in a sparse crowd of early tourists who were consulting guidebooks and peering up at the frescoes in the eye of the dome. Shayne was fifteen minutes late and Clark was noticeably impatient. He kept checking his watch and mopping his forehead with a white hankerchief.

Shayne made his way toward him through the crowd. Clark didn't look out of place among the tourists. He was gray-haired and overweight, in a seersucker suit that fitted him badly and needed pressing. His hat was pushed far back on his head. As his eyes met Shayne's he put the handkerchief away.

"Mike Shayne, right?"

Shayne nodded curtly.

"I couldn't have gone on wiping my forehead much longer," Clark said. "One of my few eccentricities is that I don't sweat." He took an unsealed envelope out of his inside coat pocket and gave it to Shayne. "Here's the list you wanted—people who rented safe-deposit boxes in seven banks, the last week in June. I have more coming. Some we won't be able to get without a court order."

"How about the terms, are they OK?"

Clark winced. "I don't object to your terms. I object to putting them in writing. I typed up an agreement, confining it to one point—if our out-of-pocket expenses are reimbursed, we will be liable to you for a fee of one-half of one percent. That would amount to fifty thousand on a reimbursement of ten million, but I think it sounds better to put it that way. Even so, it's a lot of money to commit without authorization, and I ought to talk to you fairly soon."

"I have something underway. It may not pan out."

"You were right about Wall, it seems. Toby's testifying now, and Wall is sitting there woolgathering. There were several questions he was supposed to ask, but he seems to have his mind on other things. Money, possibly."

"I'm on my way over there now. Are you—"

He stopped abruptly.

Two men came in on him from both sides. One, a solid youth with his hair cropped extremely short, said in a friendly drawl, "You'd be Mike Shayne, the well-known Shamus? Tall, redheaded—yeah, you fit the description."

Clark skittered a few steps, his eyes jumping to the envelope in Shayne's hand. The second man, a seamed, leathery individual with heavy-lidded eyes, showed Shayne a police shield.

"Lieutenant wants to talk to you."

Shayne swore viciously. It had taken them less time to identify Bixler than he had expected. After that, an easy sequence had brought them to Shayne. As soon as the news became known in Bixler's office, the girl he had had champagne with the night before, Margaret something, would volunteer the information that somebody named Mike Shayne had dropped in on Bixler at three A.M., an hour or so before he died. Shayne wasn't ready to be questioned, but he had to concede that as police work it had been fast and efficient.

"Lieutenant who?" he said mildly. "And what does he want to talk to me about?"

"This and that," the older man said. "Come on, Shayne, you're no baby. Are you licensed as a private detective in the District of Columbia? That ought to do for openers."

"OK, you deserve an explanation. I'm busy now, but I'll stop in and see you before noon."

He put Clark's envelope casually in his pocket. The first man's hand snaked out and got it.

"Who're you trying to kid? Before noon, hell. Now."

"Henry," Shayne said to Clark. The lobbyist turned reluctantly, hating to admit they were together. "These clowns can tie me up most of the day. You must have a little influence in town. See if you can get it postponed for half an hour. They can come with me. Hell, they can handcuff me if they're afraid I'll make a break."

"I can make a few phone calls," Clark said. "I don't know how much good it'll do. They tend to be a little touchy."

"You go right ahead, brother," the older man said. "And if I get new orders on the way in, I'll turn around and come back." He took Shayne's arm above the elbow. "But when I get told to pick up somebody, that's what I try to do. And I try to do it right away, not in half an hour. I'm too close to a pension."

He turned Shayne toward the great bronze doors onto the eastern portico.

"Well, it's bad luck," Shayne said to Clark, "but I guess it can't be helped. Make those phone calls anyway. What precinct are you boys from?"

"I've been patient!" the older cop snarled. "But that's all the talking we're going to do. You'll find out when we get there."

Shayne resisted the pull on his arm. He said gently, "Are you refusing to tell me your precinct number and who wants to see me? Is that the way you do things in this town?"

"You're goddamn well told that's the way we do things! No more of this crap, Shayne, or your ass is really gonna be in a high sling."

His accent had thickened, and Shayne caught an inflection that reminded him suddenly of the group of Texans Manners had brought to town. And how would the Washington cops know they could find him here at this exact moment? He ran quickly through the list of people who knew where he was—Maggie Smith, Adelle Redpath, Senator Redpath, Henry Clark, the Szep brothers. Unless he was completely wrong about everything, none of them wanted him out of action.

"I think I'll take a closer look at that shield," he said.

"I said *that's enough!*" the cop said, suddenly sounding close to hysteria.

They had Shayne by both arms, in a professional grip. He couldn't see Oskar, but Pete was just ahead in the crowd of tourists, who had lost interest in the statues and oil paintings, and were watching avidly as a big unshaven redhead resisted arrest for some unknown but certainly interesting crime.

Shayne clenched one fist, with a slight sideward movement of his head toward the man on his left. Pete gulped and nodded. He edged away and began to work back in at an angle.

"I don't like to be pushed," Shayne said. "You want to watch yourself. You're on Federal property."

"I declare," the younger man said sarcastically, "In a minute he's going to be yapping about his constitutional rights."

His face twisted abruptly and his mouth opened wide, in a lopsided O, as Pete hit him from the side, just above the pelvis. Shayne felt his grip loosen. Pivoting, the redhead stamped down on one of the other man's feet, and at the same instant wrenched his arm free and started a left. It landed high. He got in two fast, damaging rights while the man was on the way down. He was unconscious before his face hit the marble.

Going down on one knee, Shayne pulled out the police shield. The unconscious man was a cop, all right, but he was a cop from a town called Fletcher, Texas. Shayne thought he had heard that Manners had his main plant there.

As the younger man fell, Pete grabbed the envelope out of his hand and thrust it at Shayne. A powerful kick in the fallen man's lower ribs made it unlikely that he would bother anybody for the next few days.

"Let's get out of here, Mike," Pete said hoarsely.

The same detachment of Girl Scouts who had watched Shayne drink from the whiskey bottle stared at him now with real awe.

"Excuse me, girls," he said, pushing through. "Lots to do."

The crowd opened up for him; he realized that he looked dangerous and out of control. Henry Clark was nowhere in sight. Striding toward the stairs to the basement, Shayne saw one of the uniformed Capitol guards walking just as rapidly toward him, unfastening the flap of his pistol holster. The redhead didn't want any of that kind of trouble. He slowed his pace to a saunter, and Pete overtook him.

"While you're here," Shayne said, pointing to one of the paintings, "that's the Signing of the Declaration of Independence. Pay attention. Maybe you'll learn something."

"Like what?" Pete said, trying to get him to hurry. "Like it's not such a smart idea to sock cops?"

"Those guys weren't local cops."

Shayne's eyes were on the move, looking for familiar faces. Somebody must be backstopping the fake arrest, in case it went sour. And as they reached the exit between two big Revolutionary War paintings, he caught a glimpse of Stevens, Manners' huge houseman.

Shayne propelled Pete through the door. "Now we hurry."

They raced to the stairs and down to the basement. Oskar materialized behind them. An open subway car was waiting for passengers for the short underground trip to the Senate Office Building. Grabbing one of the metal hoops between the seats, Shayne swung in beside the motorman.

"Let's go."

The motorman, a portly elder statesman as dignified and imposing as many Senators he transported, said loftily, "In due time, sir."

Shayne lifted him bodily out of the way. Pete climbed over and took charge of him while Shayne studied the controls. A simple rheostat governed the flow of power from the monorail on the ceiling. He advanced the lever. They had just begun to move when Stevens burst around the corner from the stairs.

Without a second's hesitation, the big man set off along the pedestrian ramp, running at a clumsy gallop and coming surprisingly fast. Oskar yelled at Shayne, but the rheostat was already all the way over. Gradually the car picked up speed and began to pull away.

"Are you crazy?" the motorman shouted. "Slower!"

People on the ramp looked about, startled, as the car shot past. Stevens yanked out a gun and snapped off a fast

140

shot. He was too badly winded to hold his hand steady. The slug glanced from the big sign over Shayne's head: "CAUTION: Keep Arms and Feet inside Car," and went shrieking away.

Pete said angrily, "You didn't say anything about bringing a gun."

The wheels bit into the curve. Shayne was trying to find the brake. He turned off the power as he saw the brightly lighted basement lobby of the office building, and located the brake just in time. They slid into the station with wheels locked, shooting sparks.

He leaped out. Two MP's were idling in front of the elevators. One shouted, "That's him!"

They advanced, two tough-looking soldiers in white helmets. Shayne retreated toward the mouth of the tunnel, the back of his neck prickling. Stevens would come pounding around the curve in another minute. Oskar and Pete turned back suddenly into harmless visitors from out of town. The MP's called to Shayne to halt.

"I didn't do anything!" he said.

"Oh, no," the motorman cried. "You didn't manhandle me and hijack government property!"

Shayne came forward, moving carefully. The soldiers had .45's, and unlike Stevens they hadn't been breathing hard and he couldn't expect them to miss. The Szep brothers passed them, wheeled into position as though this was a maneuver they had practiced many times, and grabbed them from behind. The MP Pete was grappling with seemed to be the beefier of the pair. Shayne pumped a right into his unprotected midsection and then knocked him cold with a hard shot to the jaw. Shayne felt a searing pain all the way to his shoulder. Pete let him fall and whirled to help his brother.

The elevator arrived and discharged a load of passengers for the subway. Somebody shouted from the stairs. It was Curt Rebman, and just above him Shayne saw the National Aviation lobbyist, Henry Clark. Clark couldn't make up his mind. His face was working. But as Rebman started for Shayne, Clark whipped off his hat, reached around the

Texan and pulled the hat hard against his face. While Rebman clawed at it, trying to turn, Shayne pushed into the elevator and slammed the door.

The operator, an elderly Negro, had his hand on the control handle. Shayne closed his hand over the operator's and pulled the handle over. The Negro was breathing shallowly, his eyes tightly closed. Shayne let him go after they passed the main floor.

"Two," he said.

The old man looked around to see who was doing this to him. Shayne grinned, unsettling him to the point where he missed the floor by a foot.

"Close enough," Shayne said.

Opening the door himself, he stepped up.

"Watch your step," the operator said.

That was what Shayne intended to do. He went along the corridor, his footsteps echoing on the marble. Senator Redpath was waiting at the turn of the corridor, calmly smoking his cigar. He opened a door marked "No Admittance" as Shayne reached him.

"What kept you, Shayne?" he said.

CHAPTER 19
11:00 A.M.

THEY ENTERED A LOUNGE, FURNISHED WITH LEATHER ARM-chairs and standing ashtrays and the usual array of oil portraits in heavy gilt frames. The Washington and New York papers and loose copies of the Congressional Record lay on a mahogany side table.

"How long a recess do you want?" Redpath said.

"Tell him ten minutes, not that I can do it in that."

As Redpath opened a door Shayne heard a man's voice, mechanically amplified, speaking against a confusion of background noises.

"—be happy to answer that question, Senator. Year by year the machinery of government has grown more complex. Before I undertook this assignment from Manners Aerosystems, I will be the first to admit that I knew nothing about the manufacture of military aircraft. And the fact of the matter is, gentlemen, that I know very little about it even now."

Shayne had paused in the doorway. The big hearing room was flooded with unnaturally bright light, but it took him a moment to make any sense out of the scene. The walls were paneled in marble. There were two great crystal chandeliers. Only a stenotypist, a yard or so from Shayne, was paying any attention to the witness, who must be Sam Toby, Shayne supposed, finally spotting him at one of the crowded tables. He had a pleasure-loving face that probably rarely looked as serious as it did now. He was flanked by lawyers. As he leaned toward the microphone, he gestured with a pair of horn-rimmed glasses.

The members of the subcommittee, seated behind a curved table above him, made no pretense of listening to what he was saying. Senator Wall was reading his mail, making notes for his secretary at the bottom of each letter. Redpath bent over to whisper to Hitchcock. Hitchcock glanced at the doorway. Seeing Shayne, he frowned.

Shayne stepped back into the lounge and took the lists of names out of the thick envelope Henry Clark had given him. These were people who had rented safe-deposit boxes just before or just after the day Olga Szep stole Mrs. Redpath's diary. They were arranged alphabetically, and it took him only a moment to find the name he was looking for. He permitted himself a quarter-smile. Sooner or later, according to the law of averages, the luck was bound to start running his way.

In the hearing room, Senator Hitchcock broke into what the witness was saying. "I'll cut you off right there, Mr. Toby. We'll resume after a ten minute recess."

There was a surprised buzz from the crowd. Hitchcock bustled into the lounge.

"Mike Shayne," he said, shaking hands. "I hope the cameras didn't catch you in the doorway. This room's reserved for members of the Senate. There are too many newspapermen out there for the amount of news we're generating."

"We may have a story for them," Shayne said. "But I don't like to repeat myself, so could we get Toby and a few others in to hear this?"

Hitchcock looked at him soberly. "How important is it, Mike?"

"Damn important. A man has been killed, and a few people ought to know about it before the papers start asking them for a statement. Another thing that's happened is that a couple of Manners' thugs tried to pick me up a few minutes ago in the Capitol."

Shayne showed him the Texas police shield.

"Fletcher, Texas," Hitchcock said grimly. "That's Manners, all right. You mean they attempted to pull off a kidnapping *in the Capitol?*"

"It's not a bad place for it. It damn near worked."

Hitchcock said abruptly, "All right, who besides Toby?"

"Your daughter. Senator Wall, Senator Redpath, Maggie Smith."

"Maggie? I haven't seen her. I thought she said she had to go to New York."

He went back to the hearing room. Senator Redpath came in a moment later with Sam Toby and Trina Hitchcock. Toby's face now had a carefree expression that seemed more natural to it. He was delighted to meet Shayne. His pleasure seemed genuine, but Shayne was in hopes that it wouldn't last.

"Can you reach Manners by phone?" Shayne said.

Toby's eyes became more wary. "Under certain conditions. He's a strange man."

"I took a police buzzer off one of his boys. Another one, a big guy named Stevens, took a shot at me in the Senate subway. That's going to be in the papers unless he can talk me out of it. He's probably standing by in a parking lot, isn't he, with a phone in his car?" He pointed out a phone on the side table. "Call him."

After thinking about alternatives for a moment, the lobbyist consulted a little book and dialled a number.

Hitchcock came in. "Maggie doesn't seem to be there, Mike."

Trina cried, "Maggie! Again? I thought that was all taken care of."

"She changed her mind," Shayne said, feeling a spurt of apprehension. He had been sure she was not in danger, or he wouldn't have sent her home to change her clothes.

He rubbed the harsh growth of stubble on his chin. Telling them he would return in a moment, he went out to the corridor and around the corner to the door of the hearing room. Maggie was there, arguing fiercely with one of the guards.

"Mike!" she cried, running to him. "I couldn't get in!"

"That dress is a great improvement."

She smiled at him gratefully, and hugged his arm.

"God, Mike, I hope this works. They're going to be a tough audience."

"It had better work," Shayne said.

Senator Wall had joined the others in the lounge. They were all talking in low worried voices. They broke off at once when Shayne came in.

"Did you get Manners?" he asked Toby.

"I got him," Toby replied. "He may or may not be here. He's not too predictable."

Shayne looked around. "If any of you people haven't been told who I am, my name is Mike Shayne. I've been retained by National Aviation to see what I can do about quieting this thing down without offending anybody important."

"National Aviation!" Trina exclaimed.

"Well, you fired me, didn't you, Miss Hitchcock? I needed a client, and National didn't seem to be satisfied with the service they were getting."

Sam Toby gave an odd little giggle, which he swallowed when Shayne looked at him. Senator Hitchcock, from a position on the arm of the chair nearest the door to the hearing room, put in, "Mike, I only called a ten-minute recess. The networks are covering this live. If we're going to be out much longer, the courteous thing to do—"

"Let's not do the courteous thing," Shayne said brusquely. "It's going to be news to some of you that an investigator who used to work for this subcommittee was murdered last night. His name was Ronald Bixler. You knew him, didn't you, Wall?"

Wall's face was gray. He was moving about jerkily, unable to hold still. "Bixler? We all knew him. Emory, you remember that incompetent little pipsqueak?—Always just about to discover something that would shake Washington to its foundations. *Bixler.* He went with the Civil Service Commission."

"I'm not sure I do," Hitchcock said, frowning. "What did he work on for us?"

"It didn't amount to anything," Wall said. "He was definitely no ball of fire."

Trina Hitchcock said, "Sit down, Tom. You're making us nervous."

Wall scowled and dropped onto a leather sofa. "So Bixler

has been murdered. No doubt that's a great tragedy to somebody. But he's had no connection with the subcommittee for years. Get on with it, Shayne."

Senator Redpath said, "I think it would be better if we let Shayne do this in his own way."

Hugh Manners entered without knocking, wearing a black suit and a blue shirt with no tie. He looked around the room, checking off faces he knew, his mouth grim and unsmiling. His eyes ended on Shayne.

"Now we have our quorum," Shayne said. "I hope we'll come out of this with a deal that will satisfy everybody, or almost everybody, but we all have to understand what we're up against. What you're up against, Mr. Manners, is a charge of assault with intent to kill, and I know some Girl Scouts I can use as witnesses."

"I've had a report on that," Manners said evenly. "I think we'd better talk about it in private."

"We've already tried that. Aren't you going to offer Manners a chair, Toby?"

Toby hastily started to get up. Manners said coldly, "Stay where you are, Sam."

"I talked to Mr. Manners last night," Shayne explained, "and one of the things he said was that he never asked Toby any questions about his methods. He could use women, or bribes, or threats, and Manners didn't give a goddamn so long as he produced. Anyway, you can't complain about Toby because the opposition is even worse."

"You're way out in left field, Mike," Toby protested.

"Shut up, Sam," Manners said.

"I think it's about time you learned how Toby got you this contract," Shayne said. "It starts a year ago, when an investigator named Bixler got wind of a certain diary. He figured that if he could get that diary in his possession long enough to make a copy, he'd end up rich. But somebody on the subcommittee or the subcommittee's staff found out what he was working on and had the same idea, and Bixler found himself in Chicago with a much better job. He didn't think there was anything strange about this. He knew he deserved a promotion. Somebody else then took over the diary operation."

"Can you prove any of this?" Wall demanded.

"Hell, no," Shayne said pleasantly. "And that's my problem. The maid who actually stole the diary thought she was doing it for Bixler. All the arrangements were made by phone. Now. One of the people who had a good reason for not wanting this diary to be leaked to the papers was an Air Force colonel named Oulihan. One of the things I intend to do is get him busted out of the Air Force. I think he's the son of a bitch who put a couple of MP's on me. Make a note of that, somebody. Bust Oulihan, and I'll feel more cooperative about everything else. Oulihan happened to be in a key position in this contract competition. Manners had put in a bid, but you didn't stand much of a chance, did you, Manners?"

"Not at that time, no."

Toby said, "And that's a big objection to this theory, Shayne. Not that I admit a damn thing, but Manners was too broke to make any kind of substantial payoff. One of the things I'm known for is not doing anything like that on speculation."

"He paid off in stock," Shayne said impatiently. "He'd jump at the chance. It was like shooting craps with play money, when everybody else is using real bills. His stock was trading at less than ten bucks a share. If the contract didn't come through, it wouldn't be worth a nickel. He'd be glad to lay out ten thousand shares. If it didn't work, he wouldn't be any worse off than he already was. But if it did, the stock would boom, and he wouldn't have to hide any huge cash pay-out in his books. How's the market this morning, anybody know?"

"We opened at a hundred and fourteen," Manners said.

"Ten thousand shares times one hundred and fourteen— that's over a million bucks. And the wonderful thing about it is that everybody stood to benefit, not just the blackmailer. Even Oulihan probably was smart enough to go into the market to pick up a few thousand shares. Toby had to let go of the stock Manners gave him, but I know

148

it's done wonders for his reputation as a wizard. The only person who wasn't happy was Bixler. He'd never forgotten that old case he'd been pulled off of. He got himself transferred back to Washington and hunted up the maid who'd told him about the diary in the first place. When I bumped into him last night, he was drunk and talkative. I don't know how much of what he told me was true. He said he'd sold the maid's address to Wall, for example, for a sum in excess of two thousand bucks. True or false? Who knows?"

"And of course you can't give him a lie-detector test because he's dead," Wall commented.

Shayne nodded somberly. "The same thing goes for my other big piece of evidence. Bixler was killed near an after-hours bar on Laruc Place, and I know where I can put my hands on a witness who saw him getting out of a black and white hardtop. If this witness was sober and churchgoing and a good credit risk, I'd be in clover, but he's actually a neighborhood drunk, and I'd hate to think how a defense lawyer could cut him up on cross-examination."

"I own a black and white hardtop," Wall said, "as I'm sure you know, Shayne. There must be thousands in the city. Anything else?"

"Well, you fit most of the requirements I've been looking for, Senator. You could have found out what Bixler was up to last year, and it wouldn't be hard for you to get him shifted to that Civil Service job. You're ambitious and tough and you're willing to cut corners and you like money. Your National Aviation connection would give you the ideal cover. I asked Redpath what he thought of you in this role, and he said it was impossible because you were such a loyal National man. But Henry Clark tells me he's suddenly beginning to have doubts about your loyalty. You were out till God knows when last night, and if you thought Bixler was a real threat to that million dollars and your job in the Senate, I think you're capable of killing him. But there's only one way we could ever prove anything against you, and that's by finding those ten thousand shares of Manners' stock."

His eyes were boring into Wall's. "I have a man going through your rooms at the Park Plaza. Don't be alarmed—he won't harm anything. If he doesn't find anything there, he'll try a couple of others. Mrs. Redpath, Sam Toby, Trina Hitchcock. Somebody has that stock, and whoever has it is the murderer. Now, I think Maggie Smith has something she wants to say."

Maggie smiled brightly as the faces turned toward her. She was holding her bag too tightly, Shayne noticed, but that was her only sign of stage fright.

"It's not really conclusive," she said. "Two weeks ago I was called into the office of a certain investigative agency. Well, I suppose I can tell you—it was the FBI. I was told that Senator Wall's financial affairs were under investigation."

Wall walked up to her and gave her a piercing look. She met it without flinching.

"I'll go on, Senator, if you'll back away. I'm not at my best when people are breathing on me."

He moved off with an angry exclamation.

She continued, "They knew that he and Trina Hitchcock were having an affair. I was asked—quite forcibly, I may say—to take advantage of my occasional presence in the Hitchcock house and plant a small electronic transmitting device, to pick up their conversations. The assumption was, I believe, that Senator Wall might be using Miss Hitchcock to control or influence her father."

"You filthy—" Trina began.

Wall's face was puzzled. "I'd like to hear the rest of this, Trina."

"The thing was," Maggie said, "it was very much of a longshot, and you couldn't expect them to put their own agents on twenty-four-hour duty, on the off chance that something important might come over. They thought I'd know when Trina and Senator Wall were together. They were wrong, actually; I wasn't that much of an intimate of the Hitchcock household. However, last night I gathered from Mike Shayne that various extraordinary things were taking place, and I kept the receiver open. And suddenly, sure enough, I heard Senator Wall. Well, what I was supposed to do was tape what he said, but I couldn't get the miserable recorder to function. I'm so stupid about anything mechanical. So I took notes."

Opening her bag, she took out a folded sheaf of pages torn from a stenographer's notebook. "I got as much as I could, but my shorthand is terrible rusty." She put on her glasses. "Trina Hitchcock's voice—now you understand this isn't verbatim, by any means—Trina said, 'What are we going to do, Tom?' And his voice said, 'I don't see that there's much we can do. Let nature take its course. Nobody's been hurt so far. The profit, my God, it's fantastic. There's only one stumbling block, and that's Bixler. Something's going to have to be done about him. There's danger in trying to buy him off. He'll have an exaggerated idea about how much he deserves. And could we trust him?' "

Suddenly Trina sprang out of her chair and raked Maggie's glasses off her face.

"You're lying, you dirty tramp! The whole thing is a damn dirty lie!"

She snatched the notes and thrust them at Wall. "Here, Tom!"

Her eyes shining, Maggie clipped her with an awkward right. As Trina staggered, one of her heels broke. She tore off her other shoe and came back at Maggie, who seized a newspaper from the table and flung it in her face. It came apart, blinding her for a moment.

Then they were grabbed from behind.

Trina screamed, "Let go! I'm going to kill that bitch! I swear I'm going to kill her!"

"I'd like to see you try," Maggie said.

"OK, girls," Shayne said, stepping between them. "War's over."

"Of course she's been lying," Senator Wall said. "What interests me is who put her up to it?"

Sam Toby exclaimed, "Hitchcock!"

Everybody looked at the chair near the door, where Senator Hitchcock had been sitting. He was gone.

CHAPTER 20
11:25 A.M.

"WHAT DID YOU THINK THIS RUCKUS WAS ALL ABOUT?" Shayne asked. "Trina wanted to give him a chance to get away."

"What exactly does that mean?" Trina said icily after divesting herself of the newspaper. "He must have gone to talk to the TV people."

"Does anybody else think so?" Shayne said.

Senator Wall blustered, "If you're hoping to convince anybody that Emory Hitchcock had any part in the theft of that diary—"

"It's hard to tell what people will do before they do it," Shayne said. "Yeah—there's no question that Hitchcock is the one who stole the diary and milked it for just about a million bucks, give or take a couple of hundred thousand. He also killed Bixler, not because he's a homicidal maniac, but because he had to. Bixler was too flighty and unstable, and it wouldn't have been safe to cut him in."

"*Hitchcock*," Senator Redpath said. "I'm sorry. I don't believe it."

"I only started believing it myself at about five o'clock this morning. He made his big mistake when he didn't take his daughter into his confidence. He misjudged the girl. He thought she'd be shocked."

"Shayne," Senator Redpath said, "we don't want to be too leisurely, do we? When you said you were sending a man to look for the Manners stock at Trina Hitchcock's, wasn't the object of that to alarm Emory?"

"Sure," Shayne agreed. "And the fireworks started a minute later, which probably means that the stock is hidden somewhere in the house. But let's give him another couple of minutes."

"Will you explain something, Mike?" Maggie Smith said. "What was the point of that whole business with me, or wasn't it connected?"

"Of course it was connected," Shayne said. "Wall, for his friends in National Aviation, had begun to look into the old investigation of Toby. Probably Hitchcock had pulled everything out of the files, but he couldn't keep Bixler out of town indefinitely without calling attention to his interest in the jerk. Sooner or later Wall was going to add everything up and decide that one of his colleagues had been up to some dirty work, and had taken over the theft of the diary after sending Bixler out of town. But he couldn't conceivably suspect Hitchcock, because the old man had arranged something very clever. Maggie Smith did a job once for Toby. We can skip the details. Just because somebody does a certain kind of thing once doesn't mean they'll do it again. I've known that for years, but it slipped my mind. Toby, you understand, was the only person who had to know that Hitchcock was pulling the strings. Manners didn't know it, Oulihan didn't know it, Mrs. Redpath didn't know it. Hitchcock got Toby to suggest a woman who could be linked to some one of Toby's operations in the past, and Toby arranged the dinner where Maggie and Hitchcock met. She wasn't the aggressor in this, Hitchcock was. It was the perfect red herring, except that it worked too well. It scared Trina into hiring an out-of-town detective to break it up. She tried to fire me when she found out how much money her old man had cleared, but by then it was too late. I was a little rough with Maggie, and it didn't bother me at all. She denied it, of course. And then it struck me that the whole case against her depended on the say-so of one man, Toby, who isn't exactly famous for honesty and square-dealing."

"Now, Shayne," Toby said.

Senator Redpath said, "The diary, perhaps. Emory's always been conscious of being the poorest man in the Senate. He couldn't save anything out of his salary. He tried to get more insurance, and they turned him down because he was a cardiac patient. But *murder*—"

Shayne looked at his watch. "He didn't know that was where it would end. Everything else worked like a charm. Then Bixler came back, sold Wall the story of the diary, and stirred everything up again. Wall made certain deductions. We invented that conversation between Trina and Wall, but it probably wasn't too far off. My guess would be that Wall settled for half, which was more than he could ever expect from National. If he ever married Trina, the other fifty percent would make a nice dowry. But Hitchcock still thought he'd better talk to Bixler. To be on the safe side, he used Wall's car. And Bixler had had a hunch, which he was happy to share with an important Senator like Hitchcock. Wouldn't whoever stole the diary put the copy in a safe-deposit box? It probably wouldn't be his regular box—the diary was too hot. I found a note in Bixler's wallet. He was going to start checking the banks this morning. And Hitchcock couldn't allow that, because he himself had rented a box in the Second Federal on June 24th, the day before the diary was stolen."

"Is that where we'll find it?" Redpath said hopefully.

"Not any more. It was too dangerous to keep. He only rented the box for three months. My guess is that he burned the copy as soon as the deal was underway. He was a cautious man. And being a cautious man, he had to do something about Bixler. He persuaded him to go to the joint where the maid was working, to question her further. He made sure that Bixler was carrying plenty of cash. He could be fairly sure what would happen. Bixler had been tossed out of there before. He was drunk and cocky, and if the woman was slow about answering, as she was bound to be, Hitchcock knew that he would try to see what a little bullying would do. Of course, he was bounced by her brothers, in front of fifty witnesses, and left lying unconscious on the sidewalk. Then all Hitchcock had to do was load him into the car, kill him and dump him a couple of blocks away. Bixler had already been rolled, and Hitchcock took off his shoes to make it look even better. He didn't have to douse him with liquor. Bixler had already done that himself."

Trina was sobbing helplessly. "He couldn't have done that. My father. You don't know him."

"You didn't really know him either, did you?" Shayne said. "I think he's had about enough time."

They found him in the study of his Georgetown house. He had slipped partly off a leather chair, his eyes glazed. He was breathing heavily.

A .38 caliber revolver lay on the carpet beside him. Shayne had given him time enough to use it, but the heart attack had felled him with the gun in his hand. For eighteen hours he had been in a state of increasing tension and anxiety. He hadn't allowed himself to relax for an instant. The showdown with Wall, then the killing, the increasing terror as Shayne closed in, finally the desperate rush from Capitol Hill to burn the stock certificates that would convict him of murder—Shayne was surprised his damaged heart had held out as long as it had.

Trina ran to him, screaming. If he recognized her he gave no sign.

Wall dialled a hospital and ordered an ambulance. Shayne carried the dying man to a leather sofa. Trina covered him, and after that there was nothing to do but wait.

A dozen or so of Hitchcock's handsomely bound volumes, wrenched from the bookshelves, lay strewn about the floor. Shayne examined one. It wasn't a book, but a box disguised as a book. A heap of ashes still smoked in the fireplace.

Seeing the National Aviation lobbyist, Henry Clark, in the corridor, Shayne had brought him along. Clark conferred briefly with Manners at the far end of the study. Coming up to Shayne, he said in a hushed tone, "He's willing to give us the subcontract. Redpath says he'll set up a conference in the Pentagon and back us on recovering our expenses, and he'll see to it that some Air Force colonel— I didn't follow this part—will suddenly find himself a civilian. It looks as though your fee's in the bag. Congratulations, very fancy footwork."

"Make out the check to the Washington Little Theatre Club, or whatever the hell it's called."

"Mike!" Maggie said. "You don't have to do that."

"Don't talk him out of it," Clark said. "That's an educational contribution. That kind of check is deductible."

Manners met Shayne's eyes. Looking at the ashes in the fireplace, he shrugged slightly. "For somebody who doesn't know his way to the Washington Monument, you did fairly well, Shayne. But you were wrong about one thing. Toby wouldn't let me pay him in stock, which we would have to register under some phony name. These were bearer bonds. The price swing hasn't been quite so extreme—from 33 to 97. It's a break for us, because now the company won't have to redeem them."

"I didn't plan that," Shayne said ironically, pouring himself a cognac from the bottle Hitchcock had brought out the night before.

Redpath came over to join him. "How much publicity will there have to be?"

"That's up to you. If you try to keep it in the club, two friends of mine, Oskar and Pete Szep, will take a lot of hell from the cops. But Hitchcock doesn't look as though he has much time, and if you can get the Szep boys off the hook, I'll go along with anything else you decide."

"In other words," Senator Redpath said carefully, "if the police agree to call Bixler's death an ordinary robbery with violence, and list it as unsolved—"

"Yeah. And I'll stay around a few days to be sure that's the way it's handled."

Shayne took a long drink of cognac as Senator Redpath went on to talk to Wall. He knew he would need more than one drink to get the taste of these people out of his mouth.

Maggie said, "Will you come back to my house for breakfast when it's over, Mike?"

"No," the redhead said. "It wouldn't stop with breakfast."

She glanced at the unconscious man on the sofa. "This isn't the ideal place to say it, but would that be so terrible?"

He drank again. "It might be very damn nice. Thanks for the performance a few minutes ago. But I have to say no to the invitation."

"It's that awful thing eight years ago," she said. "I buried it as deep as I could, but I knew it wouldn't stay buried."

"It's that," Shayne said, "and it's this flirtation with Hitchcock. He started it, he kept it going, but you could have stopped it any time you wanted to by saying no."

"That's true," she said sadly. "I owe the government three thousand dollars in back taxes. Everybody's been nice about extending me credit, so now they're talking about suing me. Some days, if nobody calls me, I skip lunch and dinner. God help me, if he'd asked me to marry him I would have said yes. I'd make a good Senator's wife. Well, if you're ever in Washington again—"

"Yeah, if I'm in Washington again—"

He didn't finish. Two interns came in with a stretcher.

THE DELL GREAT MYSTERY LIBRARY
Modern masterpieces by world-famous mystery writers

THE LISTENING WALLS	Margaret Millar
NIGHTMARE	Cornell Woolrich
THE SECOND MAN	Edward Grierson
NO NEXT OF KIN	Doris Miles Disney
JOURNEY INTO FEAR	Eric Ambler
CASE PENDING	Dell Shannon
SLEEP LONG, MY LOVE	Hillary Waugh
THE LODGER	Marie Belloc Lowndes
THE PAVILION	Hilda Lawrence
THE THREE COFFINS	John Dickson Carr
HOW LIKE AN ANGEL	Margaret Millar
THE MOTIVE	Evelyn Piper
KISS KISS	Roald Dahl
BACKGROUND TO DANGER	Eric Ambler

Each 60c

THE SPY WHO CAME IN FROM THE COLD

JOHN LE CARRÉ

Now in paperback—the spellbinding
tale of espionage that became an
international bestseller!

"A great and rare treat—brilliantly conceived, faultlessly
plotted and beautifully written"—Rex Stout

"An expert thriller"—*The New Yorker*

"An inspired work"—*New York Herald Tribune*

"Both a compelling dazzlingly plotted thriller and
a substantial and penetrating novel of our times."
Anthony Boucher, *The New York Times Book Review*

DON'T MISS THESE
BESTSELLERS FROM DELL

THE SHOES OF THE FISHERMAN
Morris L. West 75c

HARLOW Irving Shulman 95c

THE 480 Eugene Burdick 85c

PEYTON PLACE Grace Metalious 75c

THE CINCINNATI KID Richard Jessup 60c

THE DIAMOND SMUGGLERS Ian Fleming 50c

HERE GOES KITTEN Robert Gover 75c

SEX AND THE COLLEGE GIRL Gael Greene 75c

THE FEMININE MYSTIQUE Betty Friedan 75c

THE COLLECTOR John Fowles 75c

THE SPY WHO CAME IN FROM THE COLD
John Le Carré 75c

CATCH-22 Joseph Heller 75c